THE CRIME: Miss Packwood, the owner of Packwood Manor, is missing. Strange that Miss Packwood disappears right after her decision to tear down the entire manor.

THE QUESTION: Who would kidnap the elderly Miss Packwood—and why?

THE SUSPECTS: *Selena and Tom Powers*—Miss Packwood's bickering niece and nephew. They stand to inherit a fortune from their aunt.
Paul Deguchi—the architect of Packwood Manor. Perhaps he wants to stop Miss Packwood from destroying his finest creation.
Carmen—the housemaid with an eye for the finer things—especially Miss Packwood's belongings.

COMPLICATIONS: Hoping to catch the criminal, Shelby arranges a surprise confrontation between two suspects. But it's Shelby who ends up getting surprised!

The Mystery Files of Shelby Woo™

A Slash in the Night
Takeout Stakeout
Hot Rock
Rock 'n' Roll Robbery
Cut and Run
House Arrest

Available from MINSTREL Books

HOUSE ARREST

LYDIA C. MARANO

A MINSTREL® BOOK

Published by POCKET BOOKS
New York   London   Toronto   Sydney   Tokyo   Singapore

This book is a work of fiction. Names, characters, places and incidents are products of the author's imagination or are used fictiously. Any resemblance to actual events or locales or persons, living or dead, is entirely coincidental.

A MINSTREL PAPERBACK *Original*

 A Minstrel Book published by
POCKET BOOKS, a division of Simon & Schuster Inc.
1230 Avenue of the Americas, New York, NY 10020

Copyright © 1998 by Viacom International Inc. All rights reserved. Based on the Nickelodeon series entitled "The Mystery Files of Shelby Woo."

ISBN: 0-671-02006-4

First Minstrel Books printing May 1998

10 9 8 7 6 5 4 3 2 1

NICKELODEON, The Mystery Files of Shelby Woo and all related titles, logos and characters are trademarks of Viacom International Inc.

A MINSTREL BOOK and colophon are registered trademarks of Simon & Schuster Inc.

Cover photography by Jeffery Salter and Tom Hurst

Printed in the U.S.A.

For the two moms in my life:
Jean Marano and Margaret Cover—
with love.

Chapter
1

I love working at the Police Station. Sure, I spend most of my time putting away files and checking to see that the pencils are sharp, but I also get to hear some pretty strange reports.

Take last week. A motel owner found an eight-foot alligator in his swimming pool, and a woman claimed her German shepherd, Ripley, was barking in Morse code. We arranged for the alligator to be removed, but could do nothing to decipher Ripley's messages. Since the attending officer felt Ripley's owner was a harmless kook, he assured her that Ripley, a shepherd, was probably speaking in its native language. The owner seemed satisfied.

Grandpa likes to say: the first thing a good detective does is eliminate the impossible. After that, anything that's left, however unlikely, must be the truth.

Still, every now and then what's left is pretty weird.

Grandpa says I have an overactive imagination, but I'll let you judge what really happened in the case I call House Arrest.

Shelby Woo began counting as soon as she saw the forked lightning in the distance.

"One thousand one, one thousand two, one thousand three . . ."

"What are you doing?" asked Noah, tossing his half-eaten cotton candy into the nearest trash container.

"Applied science." Cindi gestured with her ice cream cone.

"Huh?" Noah looked for a place to wipe his sticky hands.

Cindi offered him one of her napkins. "Remember fourth period science yesterday?"

Noah nodded absently, ignored the napkin, and wiped his hands on his jeans.

". . . One thousand ten." Shelby flinched as a huge clap of thunder reached them. "Light travels a whole lot faster than sound, which is why we see lightning before we hear thunder. Since we know that sound moves at about a mile every second, we can figure out how far away the lightning was by measuring how long it took for the sound to catch up. I counted ten seconds so—"

Noah looked up at the sky. "The storm's ten miles away." He blinked as a huge raindrop hit his face. The sky was dark with storm clouds and the wind was starting to pick up. "I vote for getting inside. Race you to the fun house!"

Laughing, the three of them rushed off.

Heavy clouds and high humidity had done nothing to dampen the spirit of the crowd that flocked to the pier for the opening of the annual carnival.

The chamber of commerce had outdone itself this year with rides and games, acrobats and jugglers. There was even a clown on stilts. One section of the parking lot had been transformed into a petting zoo for the little kids, while in another, a red-and-white tent protected the craft fair and bake sale. Young and old could be seen entering the tent, tempted by the wonderful aroma of fresh baked cookies. No one left empty-handed.

This year's profits would go toward repairing the pier's main attraction: a much-loved, decades-old merry-go-round whose sea horses, mermaids, and dolphins were cracked and pitted with age.

A large, dreadfully pale man wrapped in a huge black cape guarded the entrance to the fun house.

"He needs to get out more," Cindi whispered to Shelby as they handed him their tickets.

The man looked down at them. His dark, red-rimmed eyes and oversized fangs gave him a sinister look if you ignored the somewhat hastily applied white pancake makeup. "I only go out at night," he said in heavy accent.

Shelby giggled. "You must make a pretty big vampire bat."

"Do not mock what you cannot understand, Shelby Woo!"

Shelby stared at the vampire intensely. "Eric? Is that you?" It seemed as if everyone in Cocoa Beach was taking part in the carnival.

The ticket taker drew himself up to his full height and, fighting to remain in character, brought one end of the cape across the lower half of his face. "That's Count Eric, son of Vlad, to you!" He pointed at the entrance. "Enter mortals, if you dare."

Shelby had gotten to know Eric while investigating the theft of a rock star's costume from a window at the Cocoa Bop club. Eric was a good guy who'd unfortunately been knocked out while guarding the display.

Pushing past fake spider webs at the entrance, the teens found themselves in a strobe-lit room filled with goofy-looking ghosts, glowing skeletons, and dangling rubber bats. Spooky organ music issued from hidden speakers to drown out the noise of the carnival. Every now and then there was a howl or a scream.

The teens wound their way through Styrofoam tombstones and caskets to three doorways whose frames glowed red, green, and yellow.

Shelby read the sign on the yellow doorway: In case of panic. She grinned. "That must be the exit."

Cindi pretended to be frightened. "Oooooh, scary!"

"Do we want to go for what's behind door number one or door number two?" Shelby turned back to her friends.

Noah looked as pale as Eric's pancake makeup, while Cindi, a stunned expression on her face, pointed back at the doors.

"What?" Shelby spun around. A tattered mummy had suddenly come to life and was pointing at the red door.

It groaned, somewhat mechanically. "Take the red door and join me."

"No way!" Noah bounded through the green door. Shelby and Cindi sprinted after him through more spider webs into a brightly lit room.

Shelby giggled. "Good choice!"

The room was filled with curved mirrors. Each one was slightly different and the distorted reflections were very silly.

Cindi danced in front of a mirror that made her look short and round as a beach ball. Her head and feet were barely visible and she looked as if she could bounce. Noah had stopped in front of a mirror that made him look very tall and pencil thin.

Shelby chose one that made her look like a

pear. She did knee bends and her reflection rippled. "This is great!"

Suddenly, there was a giant boom and they were plunged into blackness.

"Okay. Maybe not too good."

Carnival sounds filled the room.

Cindi took Shelby's hand. "What happened?"

"The storm must have knocked the lights out. Where's Noah?"

"Right here. Cindi's holding my hand. At least I hope it's Cindi."

Nearby, something heavy fell over with a spectacular crash. Someone screamed.

Cindi squeezed Shelby's hand. "What was that?"

Shelby fished around for the tiny flashlight she'd slipped into the small pack at her waist—just in case. "Hold still," she shouted to no one in particular. "We don't want to break any mirrors!"

Shelby switched on the flashlight. The result was dazzling as the beam of light reflected in mirror upon mirror.

"Way to go, Shelby!" Noah said with relief. "But how do we get out of here?"

Shelby realized she couldn't see the way out.

She sensed a movement to her left. A huge pale creature with four arms and two heads lumbered toward them. It was accompanied by several other creatures, one short and wide, one ten feet tall, one with a huge head.

Outnumbered and unsure of where to run, the three teens huddled together. The creatures got closer.

"Shelby! Are you okay?" they said in one voice.

The teens breathed a collective sigh of relief as Eric stepped into the light carrying a large flashlight. All those creatures had been nothing more than Eric's reflections in the crazy mirrors!

Once outside, the teens found out that a flash of heat lightning had taken out the power in the fun house, a couple of the rides, and the bake sale tent. Needless to say, the people close to the cookies were a lot more content to remain where they were than those on top of the Ferris wheel.

The survivors of the fun house stood around swapping stories of what room they'd been trapped in and how they had gotten out. What had started as a nightmare was quickly turning into a party.

There was a sputter as the public address system kicked in. Someone who said he was Mr. Deguchi from the chamber of commerce announced that the carnival was being closed for the evening on account of the weather.

Everybody groaned.

"Oh great!" An older teen named Mark stopped bragging about how he'd knocked over a display in the fun house. "One little bit of lightning and they shut it down." He sneered at Shelby and her friends. "I guess they don't want to scare the little kids."

"What little kids?" Noah bristled when he realized Mark meant them. "We weren't scared!"

Mark smirked. "I could see that." He leaned close. "But I bet you never spent a night at the haunted mansion."

Shelby felt this had gone on long enough. "Which one?"

But Mark was not to be put off. "Very funny." He turned back to Noah. "That old place down by Flowing Well Creek. Everyone knows it's haunted."

9

Cindi was surprised. "You mean Packwood Manor?"

Mark nodded. "Yeah. The old lady who lives there is as crazy as a loon."

Shelby snickered. "Shows how much you know! Miss Packwood may be old, but she's very nice and really smart." Shelby became more confident. "Besides, there's no such thing as a haunted house."

Mark and his pals began to walk away. "If you say so. Of course, there's only one way to know for sure," he looked back at Shelby, "unless you're too chicken."

No one spoke as Cindi made the turn that would take them to Packwood Manor. It was a bit out of the way, but they had all agreed there was no harm in just driving past the house.

Cindi pulled over at a place in the road where the old stone wall surrounding the estate dipped. Beyond, they could see the lights of the house. Although it was still pretty early in the evening, the low, dark clouds and heavy winds made the teens shiver. They were glad they'd raised the top of Cindi's convertible.

Shelby peered through the window. Now here

was a mystery. "Why do they think it's haunted?"

Tree branches whipped back and forth with the winds. The sound made Noah nervous. "It's just an old house."

"We could always take a look," said Cindi, ready for a new adventure.

Shelby shook her head. "It would be wrong to sneak onto the grounds."

"Very wrong," agreed Noah.

Cindi looked disappointed.

A bolt of lightning illuminated the grounds with a cold, blue light, like an effect in a scary movie. The thunder that followed shook the car. Safe inside, Shelby and her friends shivered.

"Let's go home," said Shelby. Cindi restarted the car.

She turned on the car's headlights and prepared to pull out into the street when an open dune buggy pulled alongside. Mark and his friends leaned toward Cindi's car and cackled like chickens before driving away.

How immature, thought Shelby.

Later that evening, Shelby sat in a tree outside the manor's wall. Dry inside a rain slicker, she felt a little guilty about being there, but after all, she wasn't trespassing.

The lights had been going out one by one inside the Packwood Manor house as the people inside prepared for bed. But in one part of the grounds a small light flickered on and off.

Who'd be crazy enough to go out on a night like this? Shelby thought, then grinned as she realized she could be describing herself.

A noise from the ground below startled Shelby. She froze on her perch—hardly daring to breathe. Two people dressed in dark clothes had met, it seemed, rather unexpectedly.

"You couldn't stand it, could you," one of them whispered.

"Ha! So what's *your* excuse?" replied the other.

"I'm just looking."

They moved closer to the wall.

"Did you see those lights?"

"Too creepy."

Curious to hear more, Shelby leaned forward.

"I wish we could get a better view."

"Me too. Is *she* here?"

Shelby's branch chose that moment to bend under her weight. She tried to catch hold of another but lost her balance and came crashing down into a large puddle.

The flashlights turned in unison and trapped her in crossed beams. Unhurt thanks to a cushion of leaves, but thoroughly soaked, Shelby grinned up at Cindi and Noah.

"Yeah." Cindi helped Shelby to her feet. "She's here."

Shelby was about to explain, when a dark gray vehicle drove slowly past them. The three friends swiftly retreated into the shadow of the tree trunk. Invisible behind the wheel, the driver switched off the car's headlights and drove onto the grounds.

The next day was Friday. Shelby turned up for her job at the Cocoa Beach Police Station with the sniffles. She was also three hours early.

"Shelby! Great!" Detective Whit Hineline dropped a stack of folders on Shelby's desk. "Did you put away the file on the Bates Motel alligator?"

"Yes, Detective. You told me the case was closed."

"Well, it was. Only now there's another . . ."

His voice trailed off. "Say, what are you doing here? You're not cutting school are you?"

"No, sir. They sent us home early because of Hurricane Bobbi."

Detective Hineline was concerned. "Last time I checked it was just a tropical storm."

Shelby sneezed. "Not anymore."

The U.S. Coast Guard issued a hurricane watch when there was a nearby storm that could develop into a hurricane. That meant: be prepared. When they upgraded to a hurricane warning it meant that Bobbi had gotten bigger. If it hit land, the police would be very busy.

"I thought maybe you could use some help."

Detective Hineline smiled. Shelby was a good kid. Someday, she might even become a detective herself. "Good thinking, Shelby." He turned back to his desk. "But let's make sure you stay dry."

Shelby concentrated on the day's filing. Outside, the rain had tapered off to drizzle, but the thunderheads had turned a grayish brown and the wind was beginning to pick up.

Shelby had just brewed herself a cup of tea when a woman came in. A gust of wind caught the door, bringing in some loose pages from the *Cocoa Beach Times* and what seemed to be every fallen leaf on the block. Ignoring the mess, the woman rushed to the front desk.

"You've got to do something! Elise Packwood is missing!"

Chapter
2

It gave me the shivers! If Miss Packwood had disappeared the night before, I might have an important clue. But how could I tell Detective Hineline about the gray car entering the grounds of the estate, much less about the lights I had seen, when I wasn't supposed to be there in the first place? I decided to stick around and find out as much as possible.

Detective Hineline showed the visibly shaken woman to his desk. He caught Shelby's eye. "Why don't you bring Ms. May a cup of tea?"

The woman sat down and brushed a few leaves from her windblown hair. "Kyla, please."

Detective Hineline looked puzzled. "Huh?"

Shelby looked at her untasted tea, then at the woman. *She needs this more than I do,* Shelby thought as she put the steaming cup down on Hineline's desk. "She wants you to call her Kyla."

"Oh. Yeah, right. Thanks Shelby. That'll be all."

Kyla, who looked to be around fifty, took a sip of tea and smiled warmly at Shelby. "Perfect."

I'd never met Kyla before but her name often came up at Grandpa's weekly bridge game. She was Miss Packwood's closest friend and the two women kept busy arranging art shows, organizing charitable events, and even working to place homeless pets. Grandpa felt Kyla was a really good judge of character, which made both of the women okay in my book.

Determined to stick around as long as possible, Shelby accidentally on purpose knocked over a stack of folders. Bits and pieces of paper flew everywhere.

She glanced over at Detective Hineline and sighed loudly.

"Just clean it up," he said without even turning around.

So far, so good. She could probably make this mess last as long as necessary. Shelby worked silently so she could catch every word.

Detective Hineline reached for a new pencil. "Let's start with the basics. How long have you known Elise Packwood?"

Kyla smiled. "I came to work for her as a secretary nearly thirty years ago. But after about fifteen years, I quit."

Detective Hineline raised an eyebrow. "Why?"

"I was an initial investor in a small company that wanted to build personal computers. Sometime later, when the stock was offered for general sale, I made a fortune overnight."

Detective Hineline stopped writing. "Got any advice for someone just getting started?"

Kyla laughed. "That's easy. Think different."

The detective made a note. "So what brought you back?"

"Elise and I had become very close friends, so when she asked me to move in and work with her, I jumped at the opportunity."

"You live in Packwood Manor?"

Kyla nodded. "I have my own apartment in the north wing. The south wing is open for visitors."

"Tourists?"

"Yes. On weekends only, from ten until six."

Close by, Shelby rustled some papers to make it seem that she was working. *Why doesn't he ask about last night?*

A pair of officers came in, accompanied by more leaves. Shelby missed the next question, but heard most of the answer.

"Elise was a bit fidgety—storms always get on her nerves—so I went down to the kitchen to make some chamomile tea. I guess it was about eight-thirty. When I got back, she was gone."

Shelby touched her wrist watch. She remembered looking at it when she fell out of the tree the night before, just to make sure it wasn't broken. It had been fifteen minutes to nine.

"So what did you do?" prompted Detective Hineline.

"I went back downstairs, wondering if she'd taken another route to the kitchen." Kyla paused, re-creating the scene in her head. "The kitchen door was wide open and I could see the lights of the atrium. Elise loves to work with her plants—it calms her down—so I thought it best to let her be. After all, it's her house." Kyla took a deep breath. It looked as if she might cry. "She didn't come down for breakfast, and when I went to her suite, she was nowhere to be found! I searched the grounds, then came here."

Detective Hineline lifted the pencil and tapped his head with the eraser. "Was there a note?"

Kyla shook her head.

"Isn't it possible she went to visit friends?"

"Elise rarely does anything on the spur of the moment."

"Maybe she just went for a drive," Hineline suggested.

"Elise stopped driving five years ago. Her reflexes weren't good enough anymore." Kyla dabbed her eyes. "I just hope she's got enough insulin."

"Miss Packwood has diabetes?"

Kyla nodded.

"I have to ask, does she have any enemies?"

Kyla grinned sadly. "I don't think anyone gets to be eighty without making one or two."

Eighty! thought Shelby. *And she's still a champion bridge player!*

Officer Simpson came up and handed Hineline

a computer printout. The detective scanned it quickly. "When did this come in?"

"About five seconds ago."

"Terrific," Hineline said without conviction. He turned back to Kyla. "Who else knows she's missing?"

"No one, as far as I know."

"Do me a favor. Keep it that way. Can you cover for her?"

"I think so, but—"

"Don't worry. I'll be out to investigate as soon as possible." Hineline shook the piece of paper angrily. "But first I have to find out what idiot turned the carnival's power back on with a hurricane on the way!"

Shelby gasped. *Who would do such a thing?*

"Is there any way I can help?" asked Kyla.

"Thanks. But we can take care of it." Hineline helped her to her feet. "Besides, I have a notion who the troublemakers might be."

When Kyla reached the door she looked back at Shelby and smiled. "I hope to see you again, my dear."

Shelby waved. *Now what was that all about,* she wondered.

* * *

The winds had died down again by the time Shelby met Cindi and Noah at C.J.'s. She was bubbling over with excitement, certain that whoever had been driving the gray car was involved in Miss Packwood's disappearance.

Over a round of shakes and fries, Shelby told her friends the day's news.

"Have you told your grandfather yet?" asked Noah.

Shelby shook her head. "No. Detective Hineline doesn't want anyone to know she's missing until he checks things out."

"But isn't she a friend of yours?"

"Not exactly. I met her a couple of times when Grandpa's bridge club made it into the tournaments. Miss Packwood's a champion bridge player so she was one of the judges."

Cindi scraped the bottom of her glass with a spoon. "I was at last year's Mad Tea Party in the Packwood rose garden. It was great!"

Shelby and Noah looked at Cindi as if she had grown another nose. "So *you* know Miss Packwood?" asked Noah.

"Well, no. It was a costume party to benefit the Cocoa Beach library. Everyone had to go as a character from Lewis Carroll's *Alice's Adven-*

tures in Wonderland. Mrs. Loba, the librarian, got me in so I could take some photos for her."

Noah snickered. "Who'd you go as, the Mad Hatter?"

Cindi tried to look dignified. "I was the Queen of Hearts."

Shelby giggled. "I knew that! Off with his head!'"

Noah pretended to be frightened. "Not the face! I just got a role in the Festival of the Arts."

"The one they're having next month at Packwood Manor?" asked Will as he refilled the napkin holder.

"Way to go, Noah!" Cindi patted him on the back.

"You're in some kind of art show?" asked Shelby.

"Yes," said Cindi.

"No," said Noah at the same time.

Shelby looked at Will for help. "Well, which is it?"

"Both." Will moved on to fill the straw dispenser. "It's really neat. See, instead of looking at a bunch of old paintings or statues, you get to see live actors."

This only served to make Shelby more confused. "Huh?"

"Maybe this'll help." Will pulled out a chair and sat down. Resting his right elbow on his knee, he leaned forward bringing his fist up and resting his chin on it.

"What's he doing?" whispered Shelby.

Cindi tilted her head. "Looks as if he's thinking."

"I get it! He's posing like that sculpture called *The Thinker*."

"Exactly!" Will jumped up and slid the chair back under the table.

"So Noah's going to pose like someone in a famous work of art." Shelby spun around to face Noah. "So who, or what, are you going to be?"

Noah struck a heroic pose. "It hasn't been assigned yet, but I'm sure the festival committee will want to take advantage of my acting skills." He waved his straw about like a sword. "Maybe I'll be a prince or a hero."

Shelby grinned. "All I'm going to be is late for dinner if I don't get going. Bye!"

Shelby opened the door and took a deep breath. Something sure smelled good. Before he retired, her grandfather, Mike Woo, had been a criminologist with the San Francisco police department, but Shelby believed he could have made a living with his cooking skills as well. Now he owned and operated a bed and breakfast in Cocoa Beach called the Easterly Breeze, where he treated his guests to delicious meals.

She heard voices in the living room and went to investigate. How could she have forgotten? It was bridge night, and this week it was her grandfather's turn to play host. She hoped she hadn't missed dinner. It was bound to be something special.

Shelby greeted the club members, noting with some disappointment that the dishes had already been cleared away. Mike's guests were preparing for the first game.

Mrs. Ellison, a deli owner, shuffled a deck of cards. "Hello, Shelby. You missed a great dinner."

Her husband patted his belly. "Your grandfather always feeds us well."

"That's so we won't mind when he mops up the floor with us." Mrs. Loba, the librarian, laughed.

Mike Woo came out of the kitchen wiping his

hands on a dish towel. He noted the disappointment on his granddaughter's face. "Don't worry, I saved you some *dim sum*."

Delighted, Shelby kissed him on the cheek and raced off. *Dim sum*—meaning heart's delight—was a Chinese delicacy. Steamed dumplings hid a variety of minced meats and vegetables. Back in China *dim sum* was served for lunch, but here in America people eat it all the time. She returned to the living room with her plate piled high with *char siu bao*—large, sweet rolls stuffed with barbecued pork—and stretched out on the sofa.

Shelby often hung out around her grandfather's card games. She didn't know much about bridge, but it was a great way to find out what was happening around Cocoa Beach. Shelby considered the group one of her unnamed sources.

The game was under way. Mike and his seven guests had split up into two groups, four to a table. Mr. Fujioka, who owned an art gallery on the pier, carefully fanned his cards. "Say what you like, but I think she's finally gone around the bend."

His wife Kara grinned. "Give it up, Ray. Maybe she just wants to redecorate."

"She's been doing that for decades, but this—"

Mike Woo looked up from his cards. "I'm sure Elise knows what she's doing. If she wants to tear it down—"

Everyone began talking at once, but Shelby hardly noticed. *Tear down the manor?* This put a new slant on things!

At the other table, Mr. Peake mused, "I wonder what she's going to do with all her books?"

Mrs. Loba grinned. "Forget it, B.G. I hear she's taking them with her when she goes."

B.G. Peake, who owned a rare-book store, was only slightly embarrassed. "Too bad. There are a few beauties on those shelves I'd love to get my hands on."

Susan Peake teased her husband: "Only a few?"

The entire group laughed. Shelby remembered that none of them knew that Miss Packwood was missing.

"If you ask me, she's trying to get rid of her niece and nephew," said Mrs. Loba.

Kara picked up her cards. "Oh, Selena's not so bad, but Elise will never forgive her for marrying Tom Powers and making him part of the family."

27

Shelby felt herself drifting off. Try as she might, she couldn't keep her eyes open.

The game stopped while her grandfather felt Shelby's head with his palm. He declared it warm and packed her off to bed.

Shelby looked back at the serious faces of the adults. *Eight against one.* There was no sense arguing.

She listened closely to the adults' chatter as she rinsed off her plate in the sink. But it was too late. The topic had already changed to the medicinal value of chicken soup.

Chapter
3

I thought it was pretty suspicious that Miss Packwood disappeared soon after deciding to tear down the manor. How did Selena and Tom Powers fit in? I decided to do some investigating on my own.

Shelby rose early, despite the fact that it was Saturday. The extra sleep was just what she'd needed. Not only did she feel a whole lot better, but her teachers had neglected to hand out any homework for the weekend. She was free!

Even the weather was cooperating, sort of. Hurricane Bobbi was hovering off shore. The sky was full of spectacular thunderheads, giving everything a brown-gray color, but the air was still. It seemed as if all of nature was holding its breath.

Armed with measuring tapes and a notebook, Shelby and Cindi gave their names to the guard at the gate. They wanted to get a look around Packwood Manor before the police arrived. Shelby knew it was standard procedure to handle violent crimes and emergencies first. Since Hurricane Bobbi rated emergency status she was guessing that Hineline hadn't done a thorough investigation on the Packwood case, yet. He'd be really upset if he found her at the scene of the crime.

The security guard was a pretty young woman named Robin. "I don't see your names on the list. Who did you say you worked for?"

Fortunately, Shelby had done her homework, courtesy of Noah. "Ari Brianna. She's the Festival of the Arts coordinator from Space Coast High."

Cindi straightened the measuring tape hanging around her shoulders. "We're here to take some measurements for her."

Robin scanned the list again. "And you are?"

"Her assistants."

Robin grinned. "No, I mean tell me your names again. Since you're working with Ari, I might as well put you on the list."

The girls told her, and a moment later they were on their way to the north wing.

Cindi breathed a sigh of relief. "That was easy."

Shelby wasn't ready to relax yet. "Let's hope we don't run into Kyla."

The closer they got to the manor house, the stranger it looked.

It was a sprawling structure, three stories high and partially made of stone. The dark pitched roof gave it a formal air. It reminded Shelby of pictures she'd seen of British country homes, but there were far too many angles on this house. Stained glass windows, like giant eyes, kept guard over the well-kept grounds. Shelby counted at least two turrets.

Cindi followed Robin's directions and turned onto a service road. The architect had added fancy windows to the third floor of the east wing. A glint of light caught Cindi's eye.

"What was that?"

Shelby peered closely at the windows. "Probably a prism in one of the windows."

Cindi grinned. "It must look pretty from the inside. Especially at this time of day."

The north wing was slightly different from the east. Here the fieldstone was set off by huge dark beams. Shelby thought it looked like a crazy and very large version of an English cottage. Off to one side, a flagstone patio was surrounded by a beautiful rose garden. This was by far the most comfortable looking part of the house.

Cindi pointed to a section of the building that seemed to be entirely enclosed in glass. "Check it out!"

Shelby's eyes opened wide. "That must be the atrium." She thought of her grandfather's tiny greenhouse and the beautiful orchids he struggled so hard to maintain. "Grandpa would love that."

As Shelby knocked on the door, it suddenly dawned on her. "What if Kyla's coordinating the Festival at this end?"

"Don't worry about it, we'll think of something."

The door opened a crack and a surly looking

young woman with dark hair looked out. "The tour's in the opposite wing, but it doesn't open until ten."

The girls repeated their story and were relieved when the woman opened the door wide. "We weren't expecting you. Come on in and I'll tell Miss Kyla that you're here." She led them to the parlor and closed the door.

"So what do we do now?" Cindi wanted to know.

"I thought you had a plan!"

"I only said that because I figured you did."

"Okay. I say we stick to our story. It's worked so far."

They looked around. The room was big and airy with huge French doors that opened onto the rose garden. There was a fireplace at one end of the room and a big mahogany desk at the other. Reading lights were positioned near comfortable chairs and the hardwood floor was covered by an oriental carpet.

Cindi nudged Shelby. Built into the inside wall opposite the garden was a small window with a stained glass border. Through it, Shelby could see the studs in the wall!

The two of them jumped as the door to the

room opened again and a man and woman entered. Something struck Shelby as odd. Then she realized what it was: although the man seemed quite a bit younger than Detective Hineline, his hair had already turned completely gray. He was quite annoyed and made a big show of polishing his glasses. "Why do we have to wait for someone to come get us? When you inherit this place, the first thing I'm going to do is fire Carmen."

The woman, whose deep red hair perfectly complemented her peaches and cream complexion, gave him a dirty look. "Do we have to go through this every time we come to visit?"

"You mean every time we're summoned, don't you?"

The redhead suddenly became aware of Shelby and Cindi. "What are you doing here?"

"We're, ah, waiting to talk to Kyla," said Shelby.

"About the Festival of the Arts," added Cindi.

The woman's attitude took a sudden about-face. "Well, maybe I can help you. I'm Selena Packwood Powers and this is my husband, Tom Powers. My aunt owns the manor."

Shelby saw her chance to avoid Kyla and quickly repeated the festival story.

Tom was unsympathetic. "Why don't you come back when the tour opens?"

Cindi snapped her measuring tape. "There'll be too many people in the way. Couldn't we just get it done now?"

Selena smiled sympathetically. "I understand. Why don't you just run along. I'm sure Aunt Elise won't mind."

She doesn't know that Miss Packwood is missing! Shelby thought.

Cindi was already headed for the door. "Thanks."

Through a window, Shelby noticed a familiar character approaching—Detective Hineline! She had to get out of sight. "Would it be okay if I used the bathroom?"

Selena pointed to a door near the strange inside window.

Shelby nearly flew toward it. "Thanks. Meet you outside, Cindi."

With the door open only a crack, Shelby listened as Detective Hineline entered the parlor. He glared at Cindi as she left, then he turned to the couple inside.

He flashed his badge. "Selena and Tom Powers? I'm Detective Whit Hineline of the Cocoa Beach police department."

Looking queasy, Selena sat down behind the desk. "What happened?"

"What makes you think something's happened?"

Selena seemed to enjoy the feeling of command the chair inspired. "Why else would you be here?" Her eyes opened wide. "Is it Aunt Elise?"

"Selena, don't say anything else without our lawyer."

Selena glared at her husband. "Really, Tom."

Detective Hineline quickly stepped in. "When did you arrive?"

"About ten minutes ago. You can ask the housekeeper."

"When did you last speak with your aunt?"

"Two days ago. She asked us to come and spend the weekend."

Tom interrupted, "Detective. I demand to know why you're asking us these questions."

Hineline looked thoughtful. After a moment, he said, "We're not sure there's a problem, yet. But Kyla believes your aunt's missing."

Selena took out a package of tissues and

dabbed at her eyes. "Oh, no! I've been so worried about her. She's old and, well—"

Tom broke in. "The truth is, Detective, I think
running the estate has become too much for
her." He pointed to his temple and made little
circles in the air with his index finger. "She's not
right in the head."

"What a lot of hogwash!" Kyla stood in the
doorway. Her anger was unmistakable.

Startled, Selena leapt to her feet, upsetting a
small oriental vase on the desk. "Why, Kyla. I,
uh, didn't hear you come in."

Kyla glared at her. "Obviously." She turned
to Hineline. "Don't pay any attention to what
you just heard. Tom wants the courts to declare
Elise incompetent so that Selena will get the
estate."

Tom didn't like the way the interview was
going. "I can't believe you'd say such a thing!
We were looking forward to this visit."

Kyla's smile was not kind. "We both know
you're here because she wanted to see you. Just
as we both know there's nothing wrong with
her mind."

Selena tried to smooth it over. "I'm sure that

Tom meant to say that, ah—'' She stopped, realizing that there was no defense for her husband's nasty comments.

Kyla looked at her sadly. "Carmen has prepared your rooms. I'm sure you'd like to freshen up after your long trip." She turned back to Hineline. "Come, Detective. I'll show you Elise's suite."

Avoiding the desk, Selena sat down on one of the chairs. "Poor Aunt Elise! I wonder what she's gotten into this time?"

Tom paced. "I'm sure the police are capable of handling it."

Selena leaned forward. "Do you think we should help?"

"Oh, puh-leeze! You know you can't wait to get your hands on this house!"

It was Selena's turn to look annoyed. "And I will someday. Then, with a few changes—"

Tom smirked. "Now you sound just like her! I say we unload this old eyesore. Then we can live in style on one of the islands." His shark-like grin was unsettling. "We could even buy our own island."

"We could live in style here."

"Not if Auntie Elise spends our entire inheritance."

Selena glared. "That's *my* inheritance."

Tom quickly tried to cover his mistake. "Of course it's your inheritance, my dear. What did you think I said?" He continued smoothly. "Your aunt said she had some plans to discuss with us."

"You don't think she was going to ask *us* for money, do you?" whispered Selena.

Tom smirked. "I don't think that's what she had in mind."

Quiet as a mouse, Shelby strained to hear what was said next but her concentration was broken by a *click* behind her. She looked around quickly.

She'd been so busy hiding away from Detective Hineline, she never even noticed the room she'd hidden in. It was round, with a twelve-foot-high ceiling. All along the walls were floor-to-ceiling bookcases. A metal track ran around the room, making the higher books reachable via a wrought-iron ladder attached to it.

There was no sign on this side of the wall of the strange window in the parlor but, as Shelby tried to pinpoint the source of the sound she'd heard, she noticed a door midway up one of the cases. It was four feet high, and covered with beautiful carvings.

Shelby didn't have time to wonder what it was doing there. With another *click,* a wooden panel to the left of the fireplace swung open and Carmen stepped out. Shelby ducked behind a chair.

Carmen selected a leather-bound volume from a small reading table. Unaware of the piece of paper that had fallen from it, she tucked the book under her arm and left. As soon as she was gone, Shelby hurried to pick the paper up.

Moments later, one of the bookcases swung open and Shelby heard a now-familiar voice. "There are three or four ways into every room."

There was no time to hide. Shelby shoved the note into her pocket without reading it just as Kyla and Detective Hineline stepped into the room. The case swung closed behind them.

Detective Hineline didn't seem pleased to see Shelby. "What are you doing here?"

Shelby's mind raced. *This was bad!*

To Shelby's surprise Kyla came to her rescue. "Oh, Shelby's just here to pick up one of her grandfather's books on bridge that Elise borrowed." She turned to Shelby. "Are you having any luck, dear?"

Shelby felt she was smiling like a Cheshire cat. "No, Kyla."

Kyla pointed to the reading table. "I think I saw it on that table." She took Detective Hineline's arm. "The parlor should be free now. There are some papers in Elise's desk I think you'll want to see."

As she reached the door to the parlor she turned around and winked at Shelby!

Chapter
4

I could have spent weeks in that library, maybe even years, but I had to settle for ten minutes. More than that, Detective Hineline would have become suspicious. What was going on with Kyla? Had she seen me put the piece of paper in my pocket? Could it be that she wanted me there? Why?

The ride to C.J.'s seemed incredibly long. Shelby and Cindi were bubbling over with information, but had agreed to wait until they met up with Noah.

It was only nine-thirty, so they kept their

breakfast orders light and got right down to business.

Cindi had spotted a car that looked like the one they'd seen the night before. "No one knew who it belonged to, but one guy who left late said he had heard a car pull in about nine."

Something kept bothering Shelby. "How did the driver get onto the estate?"

Cindi was prepared. "It'd be easy if you had the security code."

Noah stirred his shake. "Then the driver would have to be someone Miss Packwood knows."

But there was another possibility and it made Shelby nervous. "Unless someone gave it to him or her."

They let that sink in. Noah was the first to recover. "What about the lights we saw?"

"Well, I think I found the tree Shelby fell out of. And as far as I can tell, they came from the direction of the atrium."

Noah spoke up. "So it could have been Miss Packwood."

"Or the kidnapper." Shelby whispered.

Cindi looked surprised. "Is that what you think happened to her?"

By now, Shelby was on a roll. "Look at the evidence. A car drives onto an estate in the middle of the night and the next morning a woman turns up missing."

Noah applauded. "Way to go Shelby! Now all we have to do is figure out who did it."

She turned the idea over in her mind. *Okay, so it wasn't the middle of the night, but it sounded more dramatic this way. Besides, it was possible.* "First, we're going to need a lot more evidence."

Shelby turned to Cindi. "You said you spoke to a worker. Is there construction going on?"

Over at the counter, Will snickered. "Yeah. For about for five decades."

Shelby was puzzled. "That's weird."

Struggling to make his share of the bill, Noah grinned. "Yeah, how can she afford to pay for all of that construction?"

Will grinned. "I heard her father made a lot of money in the twenties. He was a famous bootlegger."

"Where do you get your information, Will?"

"That's easy. I took the tour."

Shelby, Cindi, and Noah looked at each other and laughed. If it had been any more obvious, it would have bitten them. They could go on the tour!

Shelby sighed. "Someone still has to check out the atrium." She looked at Noah. "Can you do it?"

Noah sighed. "I guess so. But couldn't one of you do it?"

"We can't afford to run into Detective Hineline again," Shelby pointed out.

"And besides," Cindi was quick to add, "you're the best actor. You can play the student looking for extra work."

Noah was already thinking about the role. "Yeah, I can relate to that, but I'll have to prepare."

Shelby rolled her eyes. Noah shouldn't need to rehearse. He was always looking for extra work.

The chase was on and Cindi was becoming excited. "What's my assignment?"

Shelby handed her the paper she'd found in the library. "Why don't you see what you can find out about this."

It was a letter from Bill Deguchi of the chamber of commerce urging Miss Packwood to sell the manor to a land developer named Lawrence

Koven. Scrawled across the letter was one word: Never!

Koven Industries occupied the top floor of a modern high-rise. As she got out of the elevator, Cindi was greeted by a spectacular view of the pier and the rain-heavy clouds that stretched out beyond it. The normally blue-green water was a dark blue-gray, broken only by whitecaps.

"Looks as if Hurricane Bobbi's not through with us yet," said a deep voice behind her.

Cindi spun around. The dark, nice-looking man smiled. "I didn't mean to startle you, Miss Ornette. We spoke on the phone. I'm Mr. Koven's associate, Ali."

He offered Cindi a chair. "I think it's wonderful that someone from Space Coast High wants to do an article on Koven Industries. We're one of the major developers of indoor shopping malls in this country."

Cindi had little to go on, so she decided to get Ali to do most of the talking. "I chose it as my project for career day."

"As I explained to you, Mr. Koven is still in Los Angeles, but I'm sure I can answer any questions you have."

An architectural model on a large table caught Cindi's eye. It was pretty cool. There were a lot of white buildings neatly arranged like a wagon wheel. In the middle was a court filled with fountains and trees. Tiny plastic figures represented shoppers "Can I take a few photos of that?"

"Sure, go right ahead. It's a scale model of our next project, the Cocoa Beach Mega-Mall."

Cindi snapped a shot of the model then turned to a map on the wall. A large shaded area was broken by a big white splotch. "What's that?"

The developer pointed to the shaded area. "It represents the property we've arranged to buy."

"What's the matter with that one?"

Ali's smile became somewhat drawn. Why had he agreed to this meeting? "We're still working on that parcel. The old woman who owns it feels her house is something special." He leaned forward as if to share a secret. "But our sources say all that may change."

Cindi blinked. The parcel was Packwood Manor. "So what'll happen if you can't get her to sell?"

The developer shrugged. "At this point in the game, we haven't bought any land, so we'll just move the project." He looked at the model with pride. "It won't be hard to find a city that wants to invest in its future."

"Couldn't you build around the property?"

"We considered it, but where would we put the twenty-five-screen movie complex?"

Meanwhile, I was at Packwood Manor. The visitors' guides we kept at the Easterly Breeze made the tour sound like a lot of fun. But what I experienced was more like the scary part of a fun house.

The girl behind the counter smiled in a bored sort of way and handed Shelby a ticket. "The next tour starts at eleven. Just go through the gift shop and turn at the stairs."

Shelby looked at her watch. She had twenty minutes to kill. Hanging around the gift shop wasn't exactly what she had in mind, but maybe she'd find something there that would help her investigation.

The shop was filled with the normal assort-ment of tourist stuff, from maps of the Space Coast to dolphin-shaped sun catchers. Shelby bought a package of saltwater taffy and took her time looking around. Along one wall were photos of the early days of the manor. It'd only had one wing then, but it seemed more of a fortress.

Shelby felt a prickling on her neck, as if someone was watching her. She looked around. A young man leaned against a bookcase trying hard to look as if he was engrossed in a book. Shelby smiled at him but he looked away immediately. She glanced back at him. He seemed about twenty-eight and was good looking, but he lacked the tan of a Florida native. She pegged him as a shy tourist. Then she noticed his shoes—oxfords. Shelby grinned. *Security.*

The clerk answered the phone and nodded to the young man, who walked out. Shelby moved over to the case, eager to see what he'd been almost looking at. One book had been shoved back onto the shelf upside down. It was called *A Short History of Packwood Manor.* Shelby bought it immediately and left.

She found herself in an open courtyard. A small group of people had gathered for the start of the next tour. Normally, Shelby would have joined in the conversation, testing her ability to figure out where everyone was from without coming right out and asking them. But today she was on a mission. She found a spot a little apart from the others, sat down, and began to read. It took only a couple of pages for her to realize that she'd stumbled onto a gold mine of information.

In 1919, the 18th amendment to the Constitution made it illegal to sell or manufacture alcoholic beverages in the United States.

Prohibition, as it was called, lasted 14 years. Human nature being what it is, banning liquor just made some people want it more. Criminals like Anthony Packwood saw a chance to make a bundle by breaking the law. He became a bootlegger: producing, transporting, and even selling liquor to underground clubs known as speakeasies.

The Roaring Twenties weren't as fun as they sounded. Organized mobs fought to control neighborhoods, often waging open warfare on the streets. Many people died, Anthony Packwood among them.

Shelby looked up from the book. The group of tourists was gone. Off to one side, she could see the young man from the gift shop. He was speaking to another man whose gray hair was hard to miss—Tom Powers. She couldn't hear what they said, but the young man kept glancing over at her.

Feeling a bit uncomfortable, Shelby hurried to catch up with the tour. She was sure they hadn't gone far.

A staircase lay between her and the two men, but it was roped off. From where she was standing, she could make out a hastily scrawled construction sign. She shrugged, she didn't want to get too close to those two anyway. Funny, she hadn't noticed the sign before.

In the other direction, was an open staircase. *Gotcha!* thought Shelby. She took the steps two at a time and wound up on a dark landing. Voices filtered down from the floor above and there was the lingering aroma of perfume. This had to be the way.

Ignoring the door to her right, Shelby raced up the steps. Suddenly the lights went out!

Shelby came to and winced when she touched the lump on her head. Who, or what, had hit her? She slowly stood up and smacked into something hard. Great, now she'd have two lumps.

Sitting still, Shelby listened closely. There was no sound behind her. She turned on her flashlight and found she was on a staircase to nowhere. The steps went right up to the ceiling and stopped. She'd knocked herself out. No wonder people thought this house was weird.

She retreated to the landing. In one corner, Shelby found a padded rope neatly coiled. She could see where it should be connected to the stairway to keep people from getting hurt. Why had it been removed?

The voice of the tour guide seemed to be coming from behind a door. Shelby opened it and found herself looking down a long, narrow hallway that slanted downward. About fifteen feet away from her, light streamed in from one side.

Anxious to join the group, Shelby entered the hall, allowing the door to swing shut behind her. Too late, she realized there was no handle on her side. Shelby grinned to herself. This place was sure making her jumpy.

Shelby hurried toward what she thought was an open door, but what she found was another peculiar window cut into an inside wall. This one provided a wonderful view of the kitchen, where the tour guide was telling the group about some of the weird features of the house.

Shelby tried the window, but it wouldn't budge. Wasn't the tour group ever going to turn around? In desperation, she tapped on the glass. Wide eyed, the tourists turned, expecting to see a ghost. From where Shelby stood, they looked pretty funny and she began to giggle. Soon, everyone was laughing.

The guide forced the window open allowing Shelby to climb through. "Exploring is against the rules, young lady! You've got to stay with the group." He tried to sound fierce, but his eyes twinkled.

Shelby blushed. "I guess I took a wrong turn."

He closed the window and locked it. "If you're not careful, you might find yourself in the dungeon!"

Shelby's eyes opened wide. "This place has a dungeon?"

"It could, but I haven't found it yet."

Dave, their guide, grinned and Shelby felt rather silly. But Dave was a pro and used Shelby's unexpected arrival to explain how Anthony Packwood had liked to keep the staff on its toes, so he built a window from the hallway into the kitchen.

Shelby glanced back at the window. With the kitchen lights on and the hallway lights off, it almost looked like a mirror. No wonder no one noticed her until she knocked.

Suddenly Shelby saw a movement and a flash of light, she realized that someone was behind the glass. A woman with dark hair stepped closer to the window to check her reflection in an intricately decorated compact.

Shelby couldn't quite make out her features but it appeared to be Carmen, the housekeeper. There was an overpowering aroma. It smelled like the small pink flowers on a mimosa tree.

The woman put the compact in her pocket and stepped back from the window, making it impossible to see her features. Had she been watching Shelby? Was she the one who'd moved the rope on the stairs?

Shelby thought about confronting her but Dave was already moving on. When she turned back to the window, the woman was gone.

Chapter
5

Noah glanced at the darkening sky. He'd brought his umbrella just in case, and it was beginning to look as if he'd have to use it for more than a prop. Too bad, too. He'd been pretending it was a cane and thought he looked rather dashing.

The construction foreman stepped out of the trailer and came over to where Noah was waiting. He was in his forties but moved with the almost catlike grace of someone who practices martial arts. He offered Noah his hand. "Steve Barnes. Are you the kid who's looking for work?"

"Yes, sir."

"What's your name?" The foreman's curly brown hair was cropped short and he had kind eyes. His muscled arms reminded Noah of his broken resolution to start working out.

"Noah Allen."

"So, Noah. What experience do you have?"

Noah launched into the story he'd prepared beforehand. "Well, to tell you the truth, none. But I'm really into growing things. My mom says I have a green thumb."

Steve nodded. "Hmmm. House plants or landscaping?"

"House plants, but I'll work with anything—I'm going to be a botanist."

"You're in luck, Noah. Mr. Willmot's looking for someone to help take care of the plants in the atrium." He pointed back toward the house. "Why don't you head over there and tell him I sent you."

"Thanks, Mr. Barnes."

The foreman grinned. "You've got to start somewhere."

The atrium was deserted so Noah took a fast look around. The glassed-in room was filled with plants. He was able to recognize orchids like the ones Shelby's grandfather grew and lots of ferns. In one corner was a banana tree. There were even some weird plants growing right out of pieces of driftwood hanging on the wall. A sign on one of them identified it as a bromeliad.

The sound of running water drew him to a small goldfish pond. He gazed at the fat lazy fish with appreciation. Miss Packwood had created her own private world inside these glass walls.

Along the inside wall was a large work table. On it was a pair of gardening gloves, a half-empty glass of water, a dirty plate, and an embroidered handkerchief with the initials E.P. He looked around. The floor seemed to have been recently swept.

"Find anything exciting?"

Noah spun around. "Just looking."

Mr. Willmot beamed with pride. "Yeah, it's pretty awesome, isn't it." He brushed the dirt off his hands and offered his right one to Noah. "Jeff Willmot. How can I help you?"

Noah shook his hand. Noah began his story again, this time adding that Mr. Barnes had sent him over.

The next fifteen minutes were awful. Jeff asked

Noah gardening questions and, while Noah did his best to answer them, it was pretty clear he knew next to nothing about the care and feeding of tropical plants. The gardener patiently corrected every wrong answer.

Finally, Noah sighed. "I never realized there was so much I didn't know."

Jeff's gaze was piercing. "Well I know that part's true. Now why don't you tell me why you're really here."

Noah froze. He couldn't admit he was checking things out for Shelby, so he said the next best thing. "I'm looking for extra work."

Willmot grinned. "Why didn't you say so in the first place? It's always better to admit you don't have all the answers—that way you can learn them." He picked up a plant and prepared to get back to work. "Got a piece of paper?"

Noah nodded.

"Leave your name and phone number. I'll see what I can do."

Noah scribbled them out, but as he handed the paper to Jeff he noticed Detective Hineline walking up the path. Blurting out his thanks, he headed out the door as fast as he could.

*   *   *

The more I learned about Packwood Manor, the stranger it got! I wondered what it would be like to actually live there. It seemed harmless, but underneath it all was something dark and forbidding. I remembered Mark's warning that the Manor was haunted!

Shelby and six other tourists followed Dave into the closet. She didn't ask why they were walking into a closet. In fact, with what Shelby had seen so far, she wouldn't have been surprised to find a door that opened into the kitchen of the Easterly Breeze.

Little of the manor house was as it appeared. There were kitchen cabinets that concealed stairs. Paintings slid out of the way to reveal windows or hidden rooms. Several small, ornate doors hung within a foot of the ceiling. They were real enough, but totally useless—except as art. Shelby counted no fewer than six indoor windows including one that was stained glass. But then, there were stained glass windows on closets, too.

The strangest thing, so far: an art deco catwalk that passed above a room that could not be entered. There were sunken rooms, raised walkways, towers, and hidden staircases. What would be next?

As if in answer, the closet door slammed shut. Someone gasped. In the dim light, Shelby saw Dave smile mischievously. Suddenly, the floor beneath them seemed to drop.

Closets don't move, thought Shelby. "We're in an elevator!"

Dave nodded. "Correct. This is one of five elevators in Packwood Manor."

They came to a stop. "You're about to meet the architectural genius responsible for the wonders you've seen today."

The door re-opened on a well-lit office filled with large drafting tables, filing cabinets, and computers. It was hard to believe they were underground.

An older man looked up from his drafting table. "Right on time, Dave." What was left of his hair was totally white, but his eyes were sharp and full of life.

He handed a drawing to a younger man and stood up. Dave introduced him to the group as Paul Deguchi, chief architect. He was charming, but made it pretty clear that he needed to return to work. "Miss Packwood has suggested some major construction and we're in a critical stage of planning."

Major construction? Shelby thought. *From what I've heard it's more like major destruction!*

Shelby glanced around. Three men and two women were hard at work on various projects. Although they kept their conversation down so as not to interfere with the tour, they seemed to be a happy lot. Were they aware of Miss Packwood's plans?

Shelby's speculations were cut short by a ringing telephone. As Mr. Deguchi answered it, she saw one of the assistants lob a wadded-up piece of paper at one of his co-workers. *Well, if they know, it doesn't seem to be bothering them much.*

The architect's tone changed, obviously in reaction to something the caller had said. "I don't care what you've heard, Bill, it's *her* decision. No. No! It's not like that at all. Go ahead and have your meeting." He hung up.

Somewhat embarrassed, Mr. Deguchi turned back to the tour group. "Please excuse the interruption. My son appears to have arrived at that awkward age of thirty-five going on seven."

The older members of the group smiled.

Mr. Deguchi launched into his rehearsed talk on the manor's history. "The original house was designed in the 1920s." He casually pointed to an old photo on the wall. "But the house has been under continuous renovation since the 1940s, when Elise Packwood suddenly inherited it."

Shelby followed as he pointed out various photos of the estate taken over the decades. "Over one hundred craftsmen have toiled to continue Miss Packwood's somewhat whimsical idea of a comfortable estate. In fact, a number of the workers today are children of the original craftsmen." *Talk about continuing the family trade!* Shelby thought.

"The manor house has over fifty rooms, ten staircases, some of which actually allow passage between floors, and five elevators. There are two basements and three kitchens. The stained glass was imported from France, as were the gargoyles on the turrets."

It soon became clear that Mr. Deguchi had great pride in the house and a good deal of affection for the woman whose drive kept it going. Shelby doubted that he even knew Miss Packwood was missing.

"If the weather allows it, Dave will show you the Victorian maze in the gardens. Don't forget to come back for the Festival of the Arts next month."

It took me a few moments to connect the name, but then I had it! The architect's son was Bill Deguchi, head of the chamber of commerce. It was Bill who had written that note to Miss Packwood. Did he know what had happened to her?

Shelby left the manor house with a lot of answers and even more questions. She ran down the list in her head.

On Thursday night, when Miss Packwood disappeared, Shelby and her friends saw a dark gray car drive onto the Packwood estate with its lights out. The driver must have had the security code to get in.

A spry eighty-year-old, Miss Packwood was still active in community affairs and ran the estate herself. She had diabetes and took insulin. Would she have enough of the medication? Her reflexes weren't good enough to let her drive, but her mind was sharp—although she definitely had some weird ideas about decorating. She liked tea and plants, played bridge and collected books. She hated the man her niece married.

Were Selena and Tom holding out on the police?

Selena, Miss Packwood's neice and heir, seemed to genuinely care about her aunt, but she was very possessive about Packwood Manor and everything in it. Shelby wondered if she had a running inventory of the house's contents in her head.

Her husband, Tom Powers, had no love for his wife's aunt and would like to see her declared incompetent so he could sell the estate. He and Selena owned a dark gray sedan. Shelby had been there when they arrived at the estate on Saturday.

Bill Deguchi, head of the Cocoa Beach chamber of commerce, wanted Miss Packwood to sell the property to a developer. Why? His father was the manor's chief architect. What Bill proposed would destroy Paul Deguchi's life work.

And finally, there was Carmen the housekeeper. Shelby had seen her taking a book from the manor's library. Miss Packwood owned many expensive first editions. Was Carmen just looking for something to read, or a way to make some extra money? Was she the person who'd sent Shelby on a wild goose chase? Had she stolen that expensive-looking compact?

Miss Packwood had been missing for over twenty-four hours. She had to be found soon!

The wind was rising again and the smell of rain was in the air. It looked as if Hurricane Bobbi was going to make one more run for the coast.

Wondering how Cindi and Noah had made out, she turned a corner and ran smack into Detective Hineline.

"Shelby!"

"Oh, hi, Detective Hineline."

He glanced at the way she'd come. "Can't get enough of this place, can you? How was the tour?"

"Pretty weird," she replied honestly.

Hineline studied the house. "Yeah, there's definitely something strange about this place."

"The longer I'm here, the more I'm beginning to believe it's haunted."

The detective raised one eyebrow. "Oh?"

Shelby knew she had said too much. Now Detective Hineline would be suspicious about her visits to the manor.

"Did you ever find that book on orchids for your grandfather?" he asked.

"Uh-huh. It was just where Kyla said it would be."

Detective Hineline fought to keep a straight face. "Interesting."

This was going better than Shelby had expected. "Are you interested in orchids too?"

Hineline's gaze was piercing, though perhaps not as much as he'd like. "No. I just think it's interesting how a book on bridge transformed into a book on orchids."

Shelby squirmed slightly. "Oh, *that* book." How was she going to get out of this one? "I thought you meant the book my grandfather wanted to borrow from Miss Packwood."

"Nice try, Shelby. Now why don't you tell me

what you're really doing here." He paused. "You're not investigating are you?"

Shelby considered how much, if anything, she should admit to. Suddenly she was blinded by a flash of light followed immediately by a tremendous boom. The air smelled of scorched wood. She looked up just in time to see a huge tree branch, sheared by lightning, come crashing down toward her!

Chapter
6

Detective Hineline reacted instantly. Hurling himself at Shelby, he pushed her out of harm's way. She landed on the spongy ground with a loud *oof!*

Unfortunately, by saving her, he put himself in peril. There was the sound of splintering wood, and the branch came crashing down on him. At the same time, Shelby heard the sound of breaking glass, as the other end of the branch took out one of the stained glass windows.

Shelby struggled to her feet. "Detective Hineline!" She pushed through a tangle of twigs. "Are you all right?"

She was still trying to reach him when strong hands drew her away.

"Shelby, are you hurt?" someone asked.

Shelby shook her head. Tears were beginning to blur her vision and she felt suddenly as if she had to sit down. "Detective Hineline?" It came out as a whimper. She could see him under a tangle of branches, but he wasn't moving.

A woman's face came into focus—Kyla. She sat on the ground and made Shelby sit next to her. Shelby shivered in the woman's arms. "It's okay, Shelby. They'll get him out."

Selena and Dave were already struggling to free the fallen detective. Paul Deguchi arrived, mobile phone in hand, and called in the construction crew. They brought tools and ropes.

A few minutes later, Detective Hineline was freed. Carmen had brought a first-aid kit and Dave admitted to some paramedic training. It wasn't until he had examined the detective and declared him basically in one piece that Shelby was allowed to see him.

Still teary, but much relieved, she threw herself at him. He was full of scratches and mud, but he hugged her. "Are you okay?"

Shelby looked up and grinned. "You saved me."

"Yeah, I guess I did. And you can repay me by letting go. I think I have some bruised ribs and my right arm appears to be broken."

Apologizing, she let go immediately. He reached into his pocket with his good hand and pulled out a handkerchief. "Now, wipe your face. You look a mess."

Shelby looked down at the handkerchief and began laughing. Detective Hineline followed her gaze and joined in. The piece of cloth was full of mud.

An ambulance arrived within minutes. The paramedics wrapped Detective Hineline's ribs and checked out his arm. They insisted that he accompany them back to the hospital to have it x-rayed, but Hineline didn't want to leave the scene. "I've got work to do."

The lead paramedic looked at him sternly. "And how much do you think you're going to get done with a broken arm?"

She silenced Hineline's objections by pointing to the ambulance. "We're leaving in ten minutes.

Be on board or my partner, Rick, will have to carry you."

Hineline looked at Rick. The young man seemed barely capable of lifting Shelby. The detective smiled grimly. His arm was beginning to throb. "Okay, but I'm back here in an hour."

Shelby was next. The paramedics declared her fit, although rather filthy, and told her to take it easy the next few days. Shelby nodded. She'd have plenty of time to lie in bed after Miss Packwood was found!

She looked over at Detective Hineline. "Stay out of trouble!" he shouted.

By the time the ambulance drove away, Mr. Barnes's men had already boarded up the broken window. Paul Deguchi and Kyla stood apart from the others, speaking softly. Shelby thought they looked nice together.

Selena Powers was making sure the cleanup crew didn't trample the flower bed, which seemed kind of silly to Shelby, since the branch had taken care of most of it already. *Still*, she thought, *it's giving her something to do besides argue with her husband*. Where was he, anyway?

As if reading Shelby's mind, Tom Powers emerged from the house. "Hurricane Bobbi's changed course again." He had to shout to be heard above the rising wind. "It's picked up speed and will hit land by tonight."

The workers moved off. There was so much to do and only a limited time to do it in.

Exactly seventy-five minutes later Detective Hineline was back at the manor.

He had brushed most of the dirt and leaves from his jacket and his arm was in a cast. "I don't want to waste any more time. Is there somewhere I can freshen up so I can continue my interviews?"

He told Shelby to sit tight. "I want to know where you are. After I get this statement, I'll take you home and deliver you to your grandfather."

Selena loaned Hineline some of her husband's clothes, and the detective emerged minutes later looking a bit battered but a lot cleaner. Tom's sweater and jeans fit him well, but the way he fidgeted in them made it clear they were not his style.

Shelby laughed, but she didn't look much better. Selena's jeans and sweater were way too big for her. She'd rolled up the legs and the sleeves. It looked pretty silly, but felt comfortable.

Shelby glanced at her watch. It was still working, but what surprised her the most was the time: it was only one o'clock in the afternoon!

Detective Hineline sat at the desk in the parlor. Carmen sat opposite him, her face pale in the artificial light.

The lightning that had struck the tree was only a prelude to the thunderstorm that was now under way. Every time the lightning cracked, Carmen's eyes got bigger. She was terrified by big storms and she looked as if she was going to bolt any second.

Unable to write, and anxious to complete this interview before Carmen ran away to hide in a closet, Detective Hineline asked Shelby to write down what was said.

Shelby was thrilled. Hineline trusted her! This could be the big chance she'd been waiting for.

The interview itself turned out to be a big zero. Carmen insisted she knew nothing of Miss Packwood's disappearance. "There was a big storm so I went to bed early."

"Your room is near the kitchen. Perhaps you heard something?"

"How could I hear anything? I was asleep."

Detective Hineline decided to take another approach. "I've been told that some of Miss Packwood's belongings might be missing."

Carmen bristled. "Are you accusing me of stealing? I don't steal from Miss Elise. She is very, very good to me." A huge thunder crack interrupted her and she leapt from her seat to glare at Shelby. "You think because I come from Cuba that I steal? Shame on you!"

Shelby was taken aback. Had Carmen seen her in the library that morning? What about that compact? It'd looked very expensive.

The next bolt of lightning sent Carmen running from the room. Hineline didn't make a move to stop her. She wasn't going to leave the house. At least not in this weather.

Detective Hineline's arm must have been hurting him, because when he took me home he let me convince him that it would be better if I talked to Grandpa myself. I was sure I could say just enough to keep from being grounded for the next couple of days. I didn't have time to relax—not while Miss Packwood was still missing.

*   *   *

74

Mike Woo opened the door for his grand-daughter. "Is this a new look you're trying out?"

He was sure he'd never seen Shelby look so pathetic. Her clothes were sizes too large and rolled at the cuffs. The plastic supermarket bag containing her dirty clothes, which she'd slung over her shoulder, only added to the effect. But it was her eyes that stopped him from teasing her any further. She looked scared.

Mike knew Shelby would tell him all about it in her own way, and at her own time. All he had to do was wait—and maybe provide the right amount of hot cocoa and sympathy.

Shelby was grateful to be home. The B&B had never seemed so warm and comfortable before. She never wanted to leave. But somehow, she was going to have to get outside again. The fact that a hurricane was coming sure wasn't going to make it any easier.

She turned on the washing machine and went back to the kitchen. Grandpa had placed two steaming mugs of hot cocoa on the table. He sat with his eyes closed, but in reality, he was just waiting for the right moment to begin.

"How was the tour?" he asked in between sips.

Mike was a master of observation. Shelby's reaction would tell him a lot about what had happened today. He'd used the method many times in the field. Of course, raising a granddaughter could be just as treacherous as dealing with a criminal mastermind.

Shelby bubbled over with excitement. She told him of the stained glass from France, the tapestries from Italy, and the oriental carpets from India. She told him of staircases to nowhere, elevators in closets, and windows that looked into other rooms. In fact, she told him everything—and nothing.

"Did you see Miss Packwood?"

Shelby remembered that he didn't know about the old woman's disappearance. She shook her head. "No, but I met Kyla. She's pretty cool. I think she likes Mr. Deguchi."

Mike tried to stifle a grin, but Shelby caught it. "What's so funny?"

He finally broke down. "Kyla and Paul have been an item for longer than you've been alive."

"Wow! Aren't they ever going to get married?"

7 6

"Maybe. He's got to retire someday." He took another sip of cocoa to hide his grin. "But he better ask her soon or someone might decide to steal her away."

Shelby looked at her grandfather sideways. "You and Kyla?"

Mike tried awfully hard to keep a straight face, but finally cracked up. Shelby knew when she was being had. Too bad she didn't know what was coming next.

"Didn't Detective Hineline drop you off?"

Shelby winced. This was the part she'd been dreading ever since she stepped into Hineline's car. She thought of the story she'd prepared. It could work. After all, it wasn't really a lie; it just wasn't the whole story. Then before she knew what she was doing, it all poured out.

"While I was there, a tree was hit by lightning and a branch was going to fall on me but Detective Hineline saved me and instead it fell on him and that's how I got all muddy."

And there it was, the moment of truth. Mike didn't want to appear too anxious. "The clothes, I take it, belong to someone at the house?"

"Selena lent them to me."

"Miss Packwood's niece?"

"Yeah. She seemed stuck-up this morning, but when we needed her she was right there to help. She even lent Detective Hineline some of Tom's clothes, but he didn't like them."

"Tom didn't like his clothes?"

Shelby giggled. "No, silly. Detective Hineline didn't."

"How is Detective Hineline?

Telling the truth felt pretty good, so Shelby decided to continue. "The paramedics made him go to the hospital, because he broke his arm, but he's already back on the job."

Mike nodded. If an ambulance had been called, they probably checked out Shelby as well. He carefully avoided asking why Hineline had been at the manor. Mike knew his granddaughter too well to chalk it up to coincidence.

Shelby looked longingly at her bed. After a relaxing shower, the prospect of catching just a few winks was beginning to sound better and better. But Shelby had a suspicion that once her head hit the pillow, she wouldn't want to get up until tomorrow.

As she fought the increasing fogginess in her brain, Mike knocked at the door.

"I have to go out for a while. Will you be okay?"

Shelby yawned sleepily. "Where are you going?"

"There's a meeting of the historical society this afternoon. Elise Packwood is supposed to make her announcement." He grinned like a kid. "I wouldn't want to miss this for the world!"

Shelby was suddenly wide awake. Her grandfather still hadn't found out that Miss Packwood was missing. Maybe she could pick up something before the word got out. "May I come?"

Mike looked at her suspiciously. What was this sudden interest in old houses? "Are you sure you're up to it?"

Shelby jumped up. "Give me five minutes to get ready."

"Okay, but dress warm." Mike didn't know what was going on, but at least this way he could keep an eye on his granddaughter.

I expected the meeting of the Cocoa Beach historical society to be duller than Mr. Porter's math class. You know, a bunch of retired people sitting around talking about what color to paint their favorite park bench. But instead,

it turned out to be more like a food fight—
without the food, of course.

The meeting room in the library was packed
with residents of all ages and all backgrounds.
Normally a quiet place, the room had erupted
in shouting as soon as Paul Deguchi stepped up
to the lectern.

"Where's Elise?" One man wanted to know.

"Is it true?" shouted a woman in the last row.

Paul did his best to quiet them down. Then
someone near the back yelled, "She's not going
to sell, is she?"

The shouting began all over again. This time
the architect just waited until the crowd quieted
down on its own. It wasn't long before he
could begin.

"I was told that Elise couldn't join us tonight."
The grumbling began again but was quickly silenced by glares. "But I'll do my best to fill you
in on Elise Packwood's plans for Packwood
Manor."

Shelby looked around at the angry faces in the
audience. This was going to be one tough crowd.

"Is she really going to destroy the manor?"
asked Mr. Fujioka.

"The entire east wing and part of the north wing will be radically altered."

"How radically?"

"It may be necessary to tear them down."

Bill Deguchi rose from the audience and faced his father. "Are you saying that she won't sell to Koven Industries?"

The architect nodded at his son. "That is exactly what I'm saying."

Bill waited for the shouting to die down. "Doesn't Miss Packwood realize how much the construction of a giant mall would mean in terms of creating jobs and bringing commerce to the area?"

Some members of the audience applauded.

"I'm sure she's considered it, but you seem to have forgotten all the jobs Elise Packwood's created over the decades."

A round of murmuring followed. The volume grew and a dozen arguments broke out. Jobs. Money. The proposed Mega-Mall. Miss Packwood's right to rebuild her own home. Everyone had an opinion and they all felt the need to speak at once.

Near the front, a gray-haired woman stood up. She faced the group and cleared her throat. Suddenly the room fell silent. She refrained from smiling, but her eyes were bright. After all these years, everyone still remembered her.

Mrs. Harmon had taught history at Space Coast High for thirty years. Nearly everyone in the room who was under fifty had taken at least one history class with her and could still remember the twenty-five-page essays that could result from speaking out of turn. Even Shelby had heard stories. "I wonder if we could return to the purpose of this meeting?"

Mike Woo grinned. "She could have been a sergeant."

Shelby looked at him out of the corner of her eye. He was really enjoying this.

Mrs. Harmon spoke again. "Packwood Manor is a unique creation. It should be protected from land speculators. I propose we petition the state to make it a historical landmark."

Paul Deguchi beamed. "Thank you, Margaret! That's quite an honor."

"Nonsense, Paul," said a man in the third row. "It's a great achievement!"

"His only achievement," someone shouted angrily from the back of the room.

The architect smiled but his son stiffened. "Who said that?" He demanded.

The shouter stood up. Shelby thought he looked familiar. Wasn't he the guy from the gift shop? "Come off it, Bill. Everyone knows you think your dad wasted what could have been a brilliant career by working for someone incapable of appreciating his talent."

Paul looked stricken. He glanced over at his son, who was already engaged in another shouting match; then he left the platform. Shelby thought the older Deguchi looked very, very sad.

Chapter
7

The meeting broke up soon afterwards. I, for one, was relieved. It's always embarrassing when adults argue like that.

I thought about Paul and Bill Deguchi. How badly did Bill want that mall?

Then there was the guy from the gift shop. I'd tagged him as security, but he was awfully cozy with Tom Powers and now it appeared he knew Bill Deguchi.

My own problem was a bit more immediate: how was I going to leave the house again?

When Shelby got home there was a message for her on the answering machine from Kyla asking if she could come by around six. That gave Shelby barely an hour to find out what Cindi and Noah had learned.

"What do you mean you're going out again?" Mike looked at the rain. "What can be so important that you're willing to risk going out in a hurricane?"

Shelby was itching to tell him what was going on, but he'd be really angry if he knew she was investigating a case. "Kyla asked me to come up to the manor."

Her grandfather looked at her closely. Shelby was smart. But he had experience on his side. "Shouldn't you be lying down?"

Shelby shrugged. "Oh, Grandpa. I feel fine. Besides, it's probably something to do with the Festival of the Arts. A lot of us are working on it." She turned her back as she dialed Cindi's number. "I bet Cindi's going too."

Mike Woo sighed. He didn't believe her but there was no sense arguing. "We'll talk about this later."

Shelby, Cindi, and Noah spoke quietly in the living room. They hoped the volume of the television would blanket most of their conversation from the excellent ears of Shelby's grandfather.

Shelby spread out the pamphlet describing the manor. She ran quickly through the events leading up to the tour, the woman with the mirror, and the accident on the lawn.

"Is Detective Hineline okay?" asked Cindi.

"Man is he brave!" said Noah.

Shelby nodded. "What did you find out?"

Noah fidgeted, but he let Cindi tell her story first. "I got some photos of the model for the mall. It's going to take us days to check out all the shops. That is, if they ever build it.

"The deal all hangs on getting Packwood Manor, but the developers are really sharp."

Shelby looked at the photos. "How's that?"

"Well, their only investment so far is the design of the mall. The guy I talked to said they'll just move it to another city if they can't get all the land they need. He called it an investment in the future."

"Didn't you talk to Mr. Koven?"

"I couldn't. He's in Los Angeles negotiating another deal. I think he likes to travel." She paused, remembering something important. "His associate, Ali, hinted that they had someone on the inside who was feeding them information."

Shelby sat up straight. "Sounds like my guy in the gift shop."

Cindi nodded. "That would make sense."

Finally Noah could stand it no longer. "Aren't either of you going to ask me what I found out?"

Shelby smiled. "Sorry, Noah. I was just digesting what Cindi told me."

But Noah was going to play it for all it was worth. "So?"

Shelby rolled her eyes. "Okay, okay. So what did you find out?"

Now Noah was in his favorite role: storyteller. Shelby knew if she tried to rush him, he'd just repeat himself, so she let him tell the story on his own. When he got to the part about the atrium, she listened more intently. She was particularly interested in what he had found on the work table. If someone had taken the time to sweep the floor, why hadn't they removed the glass, the plate, and the handkerchief? And what had been swept up?

Noah took a deep breath. Investigation was hard work, especially if you're trying to make your report without stopping. "Well, what do you think?"

Shelby closed her eyes and ran through the day's events in her head. "I think we can eliminate Kyla as a suspect."

Cindi was shocked. "But Shelby, she's the one who filed the report."

"That's why I eliminated her." Shelby grinned, but she was dead serious. "We can also eliminate Paul Deguchi. He's too attached to his work and to Miss Packwood. Besides, I think he's having too much fun to throw it all away."

Noah looked confused. "What do you mean?"

"He's getting paid to do what he loves best. He'd probably continue to do it even if he wasn't getting paid."

Cindi was impressed. "Wow! What a great job."

"Exactly. Besides, if the manor gets torn down, it'll just mean more work for him and his crew." Shelby thought for a moment. "His son, Bill, is a tough one to figure out. He's proud of his father but feels his father's wasted his talents. So Bill would rather see the manor torn down."

"Maybe he just wants attention," suggested Noah.

Shelby grinned. "Sometimes you surprise me, Noah."

He blushed. "Thanks."

Shelby slipped the folded pamphlet and Cindi's photos into a manila envelope. "You know, Carmen got very defensive when Detective Hineline mentioned that some of Miss Packwood's stuff was missing."

Cindi shuddered. "Do you think she's capable of violence?"

Shelby shrugged. "Beats me, but I think she knows a whole lot more than she's saying."

"So it had to be Carmen?" Noah looked ready to storm the manor.

Shelby wasn't quite comfortable with that idea. "Let's not forget Tom and Selena Powers."

"But Selena is Miss Packwood's niece."

"And your point is?" Shelby said with a grin. "I think Selena has a good heart, but there's something about Tom I just don't trust."

Shelby, Cindi, and Noah were surprised to find the gate to the Manor locked.

Cindi was concerned. "I thought they were expecting you."

"Me too."

"How about if I park and we come with you?"

"I don't know. Kyla might not like it." Shelby opened the window and stuck her head out. "There's a bell on the left. She's probably waiting for me to ring it."

Shelby got out of the car. The rain had tapered off some, but the wind was fierce. "Come back in an hour."

Next to the bell, Shelby found a note asking her to come to the gazebo in the middle of the hedge maze. At the bottom it read: *It is urgent that I speak to you alone.*

Shelby ran back to the car. "It's okay. She left a note."

Cindi peered out the windshield. "How do we get in?"

"We don't. I do." Shelby pointed to the gate. "She left a small door unlocked."

"I don't like it, Shelby."

"Me neither, Noah, but this could be the break we need."

Cindi zipped up her jacket. She was ready to go. "What do you want us to do?"

Shelby checked her flashlight. "Wait here. If I'm not back in fifteen minutes to let you in, call the police!"

"Do you think she'll be okay?" Cindi asked, watching Shelby enter the grounds.

Noah grinned uneasily. "How much trouble can she get into in 15 minutes?"

Cindi looked at him wide eyed. "Now I don't like this."

"Yeah, what time is it now?"

I didn't know who had left the note, but the writer sounded desperate and I wanted to find out why.

Shelby pulled up the collar of her rain slicker and retied her hat. It was a good thing she hadn't brought an umbrella. It would have blown away. Still, she wished she'd dressed a bit warmer.

She followed the path to the first fork, acutely aware of the wind-blown trees bending and creaking above her head. Why did it have to be a thunder storm? The unpredictable flashes of lightning made her feel less brave.

As if to illustrate her point, a lightning bolt struck nearby. Shelby bolted in the opposite direction and found herself standing in an open field. *Not good!* she thought and immediately sought shelter in a stand of trees. She had to get inside!

Shelby had taken the precaution of putting the manor pamphlet in her pocket. She took out her flashlight and studied the map. From where she stood, she couldn't see the house. How far had she come? If she climbed a tree, she might be able to get her bearings. Of course, she could also get fried by the next blast of lightning. *Okay. Bad idea.*

An unexpected sound caused her to turn. It was the sound of a woman weeping. The wind brought the smell of mimosa. Very faintly came a high-pitched melody. Someone was playing a flute.

Intrigued, Shelby followed the sound through the trees. She used her flashlight sparingly and so was completely surprised when she stepped out of the trees and came face to face with a huge, ugly beast!

Shelby screamed and leapt backwards, covering her face. The wind whipped the pamphlet from her hands and carried it off.

When she dared to look again, she was greatly relieved to discover the creature hadn't followed her. Cautiously, she turned on her flashlight. The beam froze the beast's face in mid-growl. The fur on its back seemed to blow in the wind.

Shelby moved the light over the creature's body then stepped closer. It was a statue of a Fu Dog, or Lion of Buddha, whose fierce looks disguised its gentle nature. Its rippling fur was only the ivy growing over its back.

The statue and its mate had been placed on either side of the entrance to the hedge maze. Shelby had arrived.

The pamphlet had made the hedge maze sound like a cool thing to visit. *Maybe during the day*, thought Shelby, *but definitely not at night.*

Within minutes she was terribly lost. The walls of the maze were too high to look over and too thick to walk through. Shelby ventured deeper and deeper into the maze, driven by the need to find shelter as much as by the desire to know who'd left the note.

The smell of mimosa became stronger as Shelby stepped into the center of the maze. She'd found it quite by accident, but one look around convinced her she'd rather be anywhere else.

Enormous topiary animals guarded a gazebo: a giraffe, a griffin, a bear, a lion, a dragon. There was even a dinosaur. The wind howled through the maze and a series of lightning flashes lit up the center like a strobe. The plant animals seemed to be coming to life!

Suddenly, something large and black raced toward her. Shelby hit the ground rolling and the creature flew right over her. It smelled of mildew and moss and barely touched the ground as it disappeared into the night.

Shelby screamed and crouched low behind an enormous stone planter shaped like an urn. She knew it wasn't the safest place to be, but the thought of entering the gazebo filled her with dread. The smell of mimosa was overpowering and Shelby thought she heard someone singing. This was weird. She had to get out of here.

Her heart pounding, Shelby turned her flashlight upwards and flashed out an S.O.S. onto the low clouds. If she was very, very lucky someone might see it and come to investigate.

Chapter
8

Sometime later—after she'd gotten thoroughly soaked again—the wind brought the sound of someone approaching. Shelby hoped it wasn't that black beast returning. She groped around for something to use as a weapon. Her hand closed upon a wooden rake, and so armed, she stood to face whomever, or whatever, it was.

To her great relief a man came around the corner carrying a large lantern. Shelby shouted and he ran toward her. It was Detective Hineline!

He didn't scold, in fact he didn't even speak.

The wind was making so much noise it wouldn't have made much difference if he had. He threw a tarp around Shelby and led her out of the maze.

The house was only a hundred yards away, but with the wind and the rain it seemed a lot farther. Hineline threw open the first door they came to and they entered the relative safety of the atrium.

Shelby threw off the tarp. Something about it was familiar. She sniffed it. Here was her creature from the maze. Detective Hineline must have found it on the path.

Detective Hineline's hand radio crackled and sputtered as he made his report. "I found the girl. Continue the search."

Outside, Shelby could see a bunch of lanterns spread over the grounds as other searchers continued their mission.

Hineline swung around to face her. Shelby expected to be yelled at, but instead the detective spoke wearily. "I became worried that Miss Packwood was still missing, so I mounted a search. I just hope we're not too late."

Shelby shifted from one foot to the other. It didn't matter. There was no way she could avoid leaving a puddle on the floor. "How did you know I was here?"

He stumbled around looking in vain for a light switch. "I found your friends, Cindi and Noah, waiting outside the gate. They were trying to figure out what to do. Plus, your grandfather thought the middle of a hurricane was a strange time for someone to call a meeting. He checked with Kyla as soon as you left the house. She hadn't placed the call."

"But I did get a phone call!"

He didn't believe her. "Then why didn't you just go up to the house? Are you investigating again?"

Shelby reached into her pocket and pulled out the note she found on the gate. It had gotten pretty wet and the ink was all smeary, but even by the light of the lantern, you could still make out the words *come* and *maze*.

"This is getting serious. Why would someone deliberately send you on a wild goose chase? There's more going on here than meets the eye."

Shelby shivered.

"We'd better get you inside," said the detective.

The door connecting the atrium to the manor

was locked, so Hineline tried to raise someone on his radio. Unfortunately, the weather was messing up the reception. He decided to look for a telephone.

Shelby took out her flashlight. The work table Noah had spotted was easy to find. The evidence was as he had left it. There were crumbs on the plate. She sniffed them. Chocolate chip. Shelby's stomach growled. She could sure use something to eat right about now.

The lights came on and Shelby saw the monogrammed handkerchief. She was about to pick it up when she noticed a drop of blood on it. "Detective Hineline!" she shouted.

He came over at once. "What's wrong?"

Shelby pointed to the plate and the glass, then to the handkerchief. Hineline frowned. "Good work, Shelby. How did we miss this?"

Seeing that the floor had been swept, he got down on his hands and knees to look under the table. Shelby looked too. Shards of broken pottery had been pushed out of sight.

Hineline tried the radio again, with no result. "We'd better get inside. I need to use the phone."

Holding the tarp over their heads, the two of

them made a run to the front of the north wing. They pounded on the door and rushed inside as soon as it opened.

Shelby was shocked when she realized who had just let them in. "Grandpa!" she squealed with delight. She knew he would be angry with her, but right now she didn't care. All that mattered was that she was safe.

Kyla brought them some huge bath sheets. "You'll catch your death of cold. There's some hot cocoa in the kitchen, then we can worry about getting you into some dry clothes."

The kitchen was warm and bright. Two other people sat at the table, their hands wrapped around steaming cups of cocoa. They turned and looked guiltily at Shelby.

Noah's nose was bright red from the cold. "We didn't want to tell."

Cindi looked as if she'd been crying. "We were scared."

Shelby put her arms around them. "That's okay. I was pretty scared, too."

Mike cleared his throat. "I think you have a bit of explaining to do."

Shelby nodded, but was saved from spilling the beans by a sudden shriek from the library.

"Stay here!" Mike ordered as he and Detective Hineline raced to investigate. Kyla followed hot on their heels. And after a brief moment of hesitation, Shelby, Cindi, and Noah followed, too.

They arrived in time to see Carmen and Selena struggling over a book. Then a flash of lightning took the power out and they were left in total darkness.

Shelby turned on her flashlight immediately. Carmen was gone but Selena was sitting on the floor. She had a bruise on her face and appeared to be stunned.

"I was looking for something to read when Carmen appeared out of nowhere. She must not have known I was here, because she boldly walked over to a bookcase and stole a book."

"She was stealing it?"

"Well, why else would she take a book of poetry?"

"Did she hit you?"

Selena touched her cheek and her eyes narrowed. "She must have. Wait until I get my hands on her!"

Something about Selena's story was not quite

right. Detective Hineline looked over at her. "You stay with the kids. We'll find Carmen."

Mike Woo stepped forward. "What would you like me to do?"

Hineline smiled grimly. "I was hoping you'd ask." He drew Mike to the side and whispered to him.

Mike nodded. "I've got everything I need in the car." He stopped at the door and pointed at Shelby. "Stay out of the way."

She nodded, but her eyes were defiant.

Kyla went over to a bookcase and moved a statue. The hidden door swung open. Selena gasped. "How long has that been there?"

Kyla smiled. "Decades." She turned to Hineline. "Shall I lead?"

"Only if you want to end up in the right place," he chuckled.

Selena was livid. "Whoa, there. I'm coming with you. Stop treating me like the baby-sitter. I'm the one who was attacked, remember?"

Hineline shrugged. "Suit yourself, but stay close by. We're going to another wing." He looked at the teens. "Stay." Then he walked through the wall and followed Kyla out of sight.

Selena turned smugly. "And don't touch anything!"

Kyla reached out of the passageway and pulled Selena through. Then the bookcase swung shut, leaving the teens alone in the weird old house.

I found my backpack full of clean, dry clothes. Grandpa sure thought of everything. But where had he gone to? Carmen certainly didn't seem violent. Why had she attacked Selena? Of course, my biggest question was how much Grandpa knew about my investigation.

Hurricane Bobbi had come to town. The house creaked and groaned on its foundation. Terrible winds rattled the shutters and whipped the branches of trees. They smashed against the sides of the house in a discord of sound.

The adults had left Shelby, Cindi, and Noah well stocked with blankets and lanterns. Still, they huddled together in the middle of the room as if some force outside could reach in and pull them out into the storm.

Shelby had to find out how much her grandfather knew. "So what happened?"

Cindi grinned. "We were arguing about how long you were gone. I said it was only ten minutes—"

Noah continued, "—but she was wrong. It was twenty, at least. Anyway, this car pulled up behind us."

"You should have seen the look on Noah's face," Cindi giggled.

"I wasn't the one who screamed," he teased back.

Shelby saw this could take forever. "Just tell me how much he knows."

"Only what you told him."

Shelby breathed a sigh of relief. So Grandpa suspected that something was going on, but he had no concrete evidence against her.

Noah was really getting into it. "Wild horses couldn't drag your secret from me. No, I'd withstand any torture rather than—"

His train of thought was interrupted by the sound of glass breaking. He turned pale and put his hands up in surrender. "Okay, I'll talk!"

Shelby giggled. "Relax, Noah. It's probably just another window breaking." It really was a miracle that Noah hadn't told Grandpa everything.

Cindi looked worried. "Who do you think made the call?"

Shelby ignored the question. *What was it about this room?* Suddenly she remembered. This afternoon Carmen had entered by a secret door in the fireplace. She ran her hands along the inside of the hearth. They came away full of soot.

Noah brought the lantern closer. "Look! Shelby's invented a new parlor game. It's called Soot I Stay or Soot I Go?"

Cindi groaned. "Want some help?"

Shelby shook her head. How could she describe what she was looking for? Then she found it! Her fingers touched something metallic. She pressed against it and heard a soft click.

Shelby smiled as the left panel of the fireplace pivoted open, revealing a wooden step. Beckoning her friends to follow, Shelby darted inside. Her flashlight revealed a dark staircase that lead to an even darker area beyond.

Shelby whispered, "We're going up."

Too startled to do anything else, Cindi and Noah followed.

Chapter
9

🔍 I'd gotten us into the corridor Carmen had used to get to the library, but I had no idea where it would take us or what secrets it hid.

The staircase seemed to go on forever. Afraid of announcing their presence, Shelby used her flashlight sparingly. Unfortunately, this made Noah very nervous. He started at every sound. Once, he claimed a bat had brushed past his head and another time he said a rat had run up his leg.

They came to a landing that straightened out

into a very narrow corridor. Noah froze. "I hear voices!"

Shelby clamped her hand over his mouth. "So do I," she whispered, "and so does Cindi!"

She loosened her hand. "And if you don't keep it down, whoever's on the other side of the wall will know we're here."

Noah nodded. "Sorry."

They continued to a spot where two small holes had been drilled in the wall. Here, the voices were very clear. Shelby brought her face close to the wall and looked through the holes.

She found herself looking down into a richly furnished room. Two men were quarreling about Elise Packwood's disappearance.

The man from the gift shop paced nervously. "Are you sure she's all right?"

Another man relaxed in a chair. Shelby didn't have a good view of him, but his voice was familiar. "Chill out. The old lady's doing fine. I figure another day or two should push her over the edge just enough to get her declared incompetent."

"What about the kid?"

"She could be a real problem. If only Kyla

didn't like her—" the other man turned around suddenly. It was Tom Powers!

"What's the matter?" the younger man asked.

"I got a chill, as if someone was watching us." Tom looked around the room. "This old place gives me the creeps."

"Are you sure your wife will sell?"

"She'd better."

The younger man stopped pacing. "All my employer wanted was a commitment to sell. But we didn't sign on for any rough stuff."

Tom spoke gruffly. "Then keep your nose out of my business."

The young man slammed the door as he left.

The kids continued down the corridor. So the young security guard was a plant! Shelby wondered who he was working for. Only two people had a vested interest in what happened at Packwood Manor: Lawrence Koven and Bill Deguchi.

Noah shivered as another gust of wind rattled through the corridor. It brought with it the sound of someone singing, as well as a faint whiff of mimosa. "Shelby, where are we?"

Shelby tried to look in control, but she was

really as scared as Noah and Cindi. "As far as I can tell, we're in the walls."

The corridor ended abruptly. Shelby could sense, rather than see, a door. Beyond it, someone was weeping. Shelby took a deep breath and stepped through into Carmen's room.

Carmen looked up angrily, her eyes wet with tears. "You again! Why don't you leave me alone?"

Shelby was confused. "What are you covering up?"

"Nothing! I do not steal and I do not hurt Miss Elise."

Suddenly the regular door to Carmen's room swung open and Kyla, Selena, and Detective Hineline entered.

Hineline was angry. "What is going on here?"

Their arrival startled Shelby, but it also gave her a chance to take stock of her surroundings. The room was filled with books, paintings, and assorted bric-a-brac.

"What are you doing with all this stuff?" demanded Detective Hineline.

Carmen straightened up and looked him in the eye. "Miss Elise loaned it to me."

Selena pushed her way in and surveyed the room. "Fat chance!"

Kyla slipped through and offered the sobbing girl her handkerchief. "It could be true. Elise took a real liking to Carmen."

Carmen looked up gratefully. She dabbed her eyes, blew her nose, and the story poured out. "I came here two years ago from Cuba. I had no papers and my English was bad, but Miss Elise took me in. She became my sponsor and arranged for me to get a green card. I worked very hard for her and I told her my dream to become a teacher."

She picked up a book. "Miss Elise taught me how to read English from a book about the American War for Independence. When I read the book by myself, she gave it to me. It was the first book I ever owned."

Carmen pointed to a shelf. "Now she's teaching me about the impressionist school of art. But my favorite subject is poetry." She held up the book she had fought for in the library. "See, Walt Whitman."

Selena held up the compact Shelby had seen Carmen use. "What about this compact? Are you learning about Art Deco cosmetic cases as well?"

Carmen glared. "Of course not. It was a gift for my twenty-first birthday. Miss Elise said it had been given to her when she was my age."

She looked as if she might cry again. "It's the most beautiful thing I've ever owned. Miss Elise said I should keep it hidden. Otherwise jealous people might accuse me of stealing it."

Humbled, Selena returned the compact. "I'm sorry. I didn't understand."

Kyla turned toward Shelby. "How did you know about the secret passage?"

"I saw Carmen use it this morning."

Detective Hineline smirked. "While you were looking for the book on chess?"

"Oh, detective." Kyla put her arm around Shelby and smiled sweetly. "Everyone knows Elise plays bridge."

Sometime later, they found themselves back in the parlor. The lights had come back on, startling everyone. The phone rang just as Detective Hineline was sitting down to a much-deserved cup of coffee. Shelby still didn't know where her grandfather was, but knowing he was working with the police, she was sure he was happy. Detective Hineline sighed as he hung up the phone. Some patrolmen had caught the vandals at the carnival and wanted his help. "It's the same bunch as yesterday, I bet. Though why anyone would be out in this weather is more than I can understand."

Shelby looked over at Cindi and Noah. "Mark," she said soundlessly. Her friends nodded. The bully from the carnival would be their first guess, too.

Promising to return as soon as possible, Detective Hineline reached for the door, then spun around. He looked directly at Cindi and Noah. "Phone home!" Then he turned to Shelby. "You've got some explaining to do, young lady. Violating a direct order is a serious offense."

Shelby cringed. He was really angry with her.

"We'll talk when I get back." And with that, he was gone.

As Cindi and Noah made their phone calls, Shelby offered Carmen her hand. "I'm sorry for suspecting you."

Carmen shook it gladly. "And I'm sorry for getting you all wet."

"How did you do that?"

"I called you up and put the note on the gate. I only wanted to explain things to you, but then the thunder started and I was too afraid to go outside."

Kyla called from the kitchen. "Carmen. Why don't you help me rustle up some grub?" Carmen smiled shyly and left.

Selena had gone upstairs to lie down, leaving Shelby, Cindi, and Noah alone to pool their information.

"So what do we have?" Noah was anxious to end the investigation. This old house gave him major creeps.

"Well, we know Tom Powers is involved, but I can't see him as the brains behind this crime."

Noah looked around. "Selena?"

Shelby shook her head. "I don't think she knows what a creep she married."

Cindi thought fast. "I'd vote for Bill Deguchi."

Shelby nodded. "Yeah. The Mega-Mall could be a real plus for him politically. But how do we get him to talk?"

"Aren't he and his dad on opposite sides?" asked Noah.

Shelby grinned. "That's it! We'll get the two

of them together and see what happens." She turned to Cindi. "How's your phone voice?"

Pretending to be one of Paul Deguchi's assistants, Cindi called Bill. She said that Paul felt it was urgent they see each other immediately. Bill promised to get there as soon as he could. Forecasters were now saying that the eye of the hurricane would be over them within the hour.

Kyla came in as they were arguing about how to get Paul Deguchi to come over.

She put down the tray she was carrying. It was filled with soup and sandwiches. "Can I help?"

Shelby grabbed one of the sandwiches and shoved it in her mouth. Then, remembering her manners, she chewed slowly and swallowed. Kyla seemed okay. She decided to throw caution to the wind. "We think Bill Deguchi knows something about Miss Packwood's disappearance and we need his father to help get him to talk."

Kyla's look was piercing. She reached for the phone and dialed. After what must have been two rings, she spoke three words, then hung up. "He'll be here within the hour."

Cindi looked surprised. "How can you be so sure?"

"Because the phone line went out as soon as I said hello. He won't be able to rest without knowing what was going on." Shelby noticed how her eyes twinkled when she spoke of the architect.

She couldn't stand it any longer. "Why did you cover for me and why are you helping us now?"

Kyla grinned. "I've heard you're quite a little investigator."

Well, thought Shelby, *that makes it as clear as mud.* "Uh, thanks."

Selena came back into the room. She seemed subdued and her eyes were red from crying.

Kyla offered her a tissue. "Is anything wrong?"

Selena made a great show of blowing her nose. "Oh, it's nothing. Just a cold."

Soon afterwards, Tom Powers came stomping down the stairs holding his suitcase. Clothes stuck out from every side of it, as if he'd packed very quickly. "I'll be back," he barked as he slammed the front door. Shelby heard him kick the door and say something rude to the car. Apparently it wouldn't start.

Shelby peeked through the window. She saw Tom throw his bag at the door. He marched away.

No one said anything, but Selena looked very sad. "Oh well, at least now I know what he was really like. Aunt Elise was right all along."

As if in answer, the whole house shook with the wind and groaned. Kyla stood up. "Would you like a cup of tea, my dear?"

Selena looked up and smiled. "Make it cocoa and you have a deal. In fact, I'll even prepare it."

Selena and Kyla went into the kitchen together. When they came out Selena held a tray with enough mugs for everyone.

Chapter
10

I wasn't sure how to deal with Tom Powers's leaving, but I had to admit I was glad to see him go.

Thanks to Kyla, we'd set the stage to catch a kidnapper. But right from the start, nothing went as I'd planned.

Paul and Bill Deguchi arrived at the same time. They began arguing outside the front door and continued as Carmen showed them into the library.

Paul took Kyla's hands in his own. "The phone went dead. Is everything okay?"

Kyla nodded. "It's fine. Well, almost everything is fine, but we needed you here."

Bill looked from one person to another. "Is this someone's idea of a joke?"

Kyla glared at him. Her response was simple and direct and it was meant to shock. "Elise is missing."

Shelby watched as both men sat down sharply. *Neither one of them knew!*

Paul recovered first. "Have you called the police? When did you notice? Has there been a note? What can I do?"

Bill was still white. Shelby decided to strike. "Do you know anything about her disappearance?"

He faced her, enraged. "Who are you to question me?"

"I work for the police department." Which of course was very true, but not quite in the way she implied.

The architect rose to his feet, towering above his son. "Answer the girl. What do you know?"

Shocked that his father would question his honesty, Bill sat down again. "I'm a politician, not a kidnapper."

But Shelby was an expert at evasion and recognized it at once. "That's not really answering the question, Mr. Deguchi." She sat down across from him. "Can you tell us why someone would want to kidnap Miss Packwood?"

Bill sighed. "I just suggested to Tom that he convince his aunt to sell the manor. This way, the community would benefit and I would too."

Shelby prodded. "You mean politically?"

"No. I don't care about politics." He looked at Kyla May. "I bet you don't know that I have a degree in architecture."

Kyla shook her head and Bill continued. "Of course not. He wouldn't have told you. Nothing has ever mattered to my father except this house. It's the most important thing in his life."

The older Deguchi tried to interrupt. "Now, Bill, you know you and your mother always came first."

Bill laughed. "Is that why you went back to work right after her funeral? Tell me, Dad, how old are my kids?"

"Two, seven and eleven?"

"Wrong. Mary Caroline's thirteen, Charlotte's eight, and Sarah's just turned six." Bill shook his head. "Is it any wonder I want to see this place demolished? Maybe you'll finally get to spend some time with your family."

Paul Deguchi was unprepared for this attack. How could he explain how much this house had come to represent and why he had continued to work on it for so many years?

He began to speak, softly at first, about the real history of Packwood Manor.

"The history books will tell you that Packwood Manor was built with dirty money, and it's true to a point.

"I worked for Anthony Packwood when I was a kid. I never knew what was in the packages I delivered. I never checked. I was happy just to have a job.

"When Packwood died, the authorities went after the syndicate. Unable to lay their hands on his legitimate investments—which his daughter inherited—they went after his employees. The adults were sent to jail, and many of the kids who were used as runners were packed off to reform school.

"I was lucky. Miss Packwood made me an offer I couldn't refuse: she'd protect me, if I stayed out of trouble and got an education. She even offered to foot the bill.

"When I graduated in 1950 she gave me a job. I learned she had made similar deals with many of the other kids whose parents had worked for her father.

"She felt that we deserved a chance. She had some weird ideas about what she wanted, but it meant a steady job and fair pay.

"In time, no one remembered our past."

Paul looked at his son. "I'd hoped that someday you'd take over my job at the manor. But instead you grew up resenting it."

Shelby spoke up. "So by deciding to knock down part of the manor and rebuild, Miss Packwood was just creating more jobs for the next generation."

Paul nodded.

Selena sighed. "Everyone makes out but me. Aunt Elise is spending my inheritance."

"Nonsense! She's worth more today than ever. And besides, you'll be getting far more than just a fortune. You'll have the respect and loyalty of dozens of craftsmen whose major concern will be designing and building the house of your dreams."

*   *   *

The next few minutes were uncomfortable, as father and son refused to face each other.

Meanwhile Shelby was hard at work thinking. The answer to Miss Packwood's whereabouts was right in front of her, if only she could see it. Suddenly she blinked. "Then you weren't the original architect?"

Paul grinned. "I'm not that old."

"Is there any of the original house left?"

"You're sitting in it."

"You mean the north wing is older than the one that's open to tourists?"

"Yes. We stuck the atrium on it and gave it a face lift. Elise didn't want us to touch the hedge maze."

Shelby stood up. "Then we have to go to the source." Everyone looked at her as if she'd gone nuts. "That's what my grandpa always says."

Kyla grinned. "Well, dear, that's going to be a little difficult, since the original architect, Rupert T. Swanson, died in 1950."

"You aren't suggesting a seance are you?" Bill meant it as a joke, but Noah turned white.

Shelby looked around nervously. "I'd rather not. Do you still have the original plans?"

Everyone looked puzzled, especially Selena.

"What does this have to do with Aunt Elise's disappearance?"

Shelby was thinking so fast, she could only speak in shorthand. " 'The Purloined Letter'!"

The adults looked at each other, but Cindi spoke up. "It's a story by Edgar Allan Poe that we read last week in English. It's about a letter that's successfully hidden in plain sight."

The significance began to dawn on Kyla. "You mean—"

"I think Tom hid her somewhere in the house!"

"But when?" asked Selena. "We didn't get here until this morning."

"*You* got here this morning. Look, it's a long story, but the three of us saw Tom drive onto the estate on Thursday night."

Selena pursed her lips. "He said he was working late."

Bill Deguchi leapt to his feet. "Speaking of working late, what are we waiting for? Come on Dad, I'll help you find the plans."

Chapter
11

Shelby looked at all the papers and shook her head. She never imagined that building a house—even one this big—could be so complicated.

Paul and his son were crouched on the floor examining what they hoped would be the right blueprints. It was tough going. The years had taken their toll on the papers.

Paul was surprised to find that Anthony Packwood had ordered significant changes to the house and gardens. No complete floor plan existed, and they were unsure how far back to look.

Shelby and Kyla stayed with the men while the others gathered up all the blankets, ropes, and lanterns they could find. Shelby was sure there was something she was overlooking.

Bill put a set of blueprints on the drafting table. The paper curled so badly he had to hold it down the edges with paperweights. "As far as I can tell, this is the most complete version of the early plans."

All the lines and notations made Shelby's head spin. With so many passageways, they could be searching for days and still turn up nothing. Deprived of insulin and subjected to who-knew-what kind of exposure, Miss Packwood didn't have much time.

Suddenly she remembered. Grandpa always said, "A good detective uses all his senses." It came to her!

"Does Miss Packwood wear mimosa perfume?"

Kyla grinned. "Not that I know of."

Shelby sagged. "Maybe it was a ghost. All I know is I keep smelling mimosa."

Paul Deguchi stood with his eyes closed, as if trying to remember something long past. "It was her mother's favorite scent."

"When did Miss Packwood's mother die?"

Bill still couldn't believe they were letting this kid run the investigation. "What does this have to do with blueprints?"

Kyla hushed him up. "Give her a chance, Bill. She's done remarkably well so far."

Paul Deguchi thought hard. "It was about ten years after Anthony was shot: 1940."

Shelby grinned. "And I bet all her stuff was packed up and stored."

"Sure. Whatever personal stuff wasn't given away."

Bill brought his fist down on the table. "I see what she's getting at! Maybe Tom put her in the room with all her mother's stuff. It would have been built before her death."

Paul began digging through the plans. "It's a long shot."

His son joined in the search. "Very long," he agreed. "Almost nonexistent."

He held up a page labeled 1941. "Here we go!"

Paul laid a piece of acetate over the blueprint so he could write on it. He crossed out several passageways that had been torn down.

Shelby was particularly interested in one that

connected the atrium with the hedge maze. "What a weird place for a passageway."

"Not really," said Paul. "Remember Anthony Packwood was a bootlegger. He probably built a number of secret ways into the house. I remember when we found where he hid the stolen goods." He stopped and a strange look passed over his face.

Shelby knew where it was. "It was right behind the work table in the atrium."

Bill grabbed the blueprint as his father sprinted for the door. Kyla was already holding the elevator. "Let's go!"

They found Mike Woo in the atrium bagging evidence. He waved them over to the work table. "It's about time you showed up. Do I have to do all the work?"

A very wet Tom Powers sat on a chair. He made no effort to rise but glared at the newcomers. At his feet was a piece of black plastic and some messed up wires.

Shelby's grandfather grinned. "Mr. Powers came in about twenty minutes ago. I convinced him to wait. I took the precaution of removing the distributor cap from his car. Detective Hineline wanted to make sure he couldn't drive away before answering a few questions."

Mike pointed to the floor. "Look at what I found." Scrape marks marred the floor where something large had been pulled across it. "This tree has been moved. I believe there is a door behind it."

But the tree was huge and had been recently watered. The added weight made it impossible to budge.

Over on the chair, Tom Powers sneered.

Shelby thought about the mimosa smell. "Where's that blueprint?"

Bill laid it out on the floor. Shelby pointed to a very light line that looked as if it had been erased.

"Is this another tunnel?"

"Could be. You've got good eyes!"

Shelby sprinted out the door. "Follow me!" She headed for the center of the maze. The other end of the tunnel was under the stone urn!

Elise Packwood lay on a bundle of old clothes. Her last candle had burned out hours ago. She was cold and weak from exhaustion. Reaching inside the pocket of her sweater, she felt for the last chocolate chip cookie. There was nothing to wash it down with. She ate it very slowly, trying to make the sugar last as long as possible. Maybe help would come today.

Elise awoke in a hospital bed. The light hurt her eyes but she kept them open and wept at the joy of seeing again. There were people surrounding her bed. "How long?" she managed to croak.

Kyla's face came into focus. "Two days. How are you feeling, Elise?"

"I've been better!"

A nurse came in and chased them all out. "You can talk to her after she gets some sleep."

Some days later, the doctors declared Miss Packwood fit to answer questions. Detective Hineline entered her room to find Kyla May, Selena, Paul, Bill, Shelby, and her grandfather already there.

"Okay, everybody. Clear the room. Police business."

Elise Packwood laughed. "Why Detective, you're just in time to hear my side of the story. We're trying to piece together what happened."

He sat down, defeated with two sentences. Miss Packwood, it seemed, was back in charge.

"I'd gone to the atrium to try to relax among the plants. I brought a snack from my room and was checking out the latest bloom on an epiphyllium when I heard a sound.

"I'm afraid I dropped the pot, so I tried to salvage the plant. That's when it bit me. By that, I mean I got a spine in my finger. When I removed the spine, my finger bled a bit."

"You wrapped it in your handkerchief," filled in Shelby.

Elise nodded.

"I noticed a car had pulled up outside. It was my dolt of a nephew, Tom. He'd undoubtedly seen the light on in the atrium and had come to plague me about something."

She turned to Selena. "I'm sorry, my dear, but I really don't understand what you saw in that man."

Selena smiled palely. "That's okay, Aunt Elise. I don't either."

"I remembered the room where we'd stored all of Mother's belongings after she passed away. My father had built the room to put his bootleg liquor in. He'd hidden the door behind a Madagascar palm.

"I decided to hide out until Tom left.

"The light bulb had burned out long ago, but there were candles and a box of matches. I decided to spend my time going through boxes and remembering the past."

She smiled at Shelby and a wonderful thing happened; her whole face seemed to light up and she looked younger. "When you get to be my age, you do that a lot." Shelby grinned. Miss Packwood was still a beautiful woman.

"Unfortunately, Tom followed me. He insisted I give control of the estate to him. If I didn't do as he said, he'd find a way to have me declared incompetent.

"I, of course, refused, and he left in a huff. There was a lot of noise and then I realized what had happened. He'd locked me in."

She paused and Shelby jumped right in. "He figured that by the time he let you out, you'd be ready to do anything he asked."

Elise patted her hand. "He didn't know who he was dealing with, did he?

"Insulin wouldn't be a problem as long as I

didn't exert myself, and I had my cookies. I could get someone's attention in the morning."

"I heard talking and laughter," said Shelby. "Was that you?"

"Yes. I'd found a bottle from my mother's perfume and it reminded me of her. I played the flute and pretended to talk to her to pass the time. It's another habit of old people." She grinned again.

Shelby thought about what she'd just heard. "Then the smell of mimosa *was* from you."

Miss Packwood laughed out loud. "Oh no, child. There was no perfume left in the bottle. It was empty."

A chill ran up Shelby's back.

Mike Woo pulled up outside the Cocoa Beach Police Station and honked the horn. Shelby read her final entry on the case before closing the file.

The Deguchis were reunited. Paul has retired and, at the end of the month, he and Kyla will be married. He's looking forward to getting to know his grandchildren.

Miss Packwood is happy for her friend, but sad to see her go. Still, there'll be plenty to

keep her busy. She's decided on building another addition to the manor house rather than
tearing anything down. The Festival of the Arts
is next week and Carmen still hasn't discov-
ered the work of Erte.

Selena finally understood what her aunt was
all about. A fortune means nothing unless it
is used for the greater good. After all, how
many millions do you need? She's divorcing
Tom (who's going to be spending the next de-
cade, or two, in jail) and moving in with her
aunt. Hopefully, there'll be plenty of time left
for her to learn how to handle the estate.

Lawrence Koven returned to Cocoa Beach to
discover that his plans for a mega-mall had
been rejected by the city council on the recom-
mendation of the chamber of commerce. Acting quickly, he and Ali moved the project to
Los Angeles. Miss Packwood bought up the
property of anyone who still wanted to sell.
Bill Deguchi has been hired to design some
tasteful housing for retirees.

Cindi plans on photographing the festival
and I understand that Noah's watermelon costume is brilliant.

And me? I learned how important friendship
is. And family. And how you can turn anything
to good if you try hard enough.

House Arrest

As for Packwood Manor being haunted, the jury's still out on that one. But I think I'll do all my visiting during the day.

Case closed.

About the Author

LYDIA S. MARANO grew up in a library, where she was befriended by a family of wyverns who'd taken up residence in the mythology section. These fearsome, intelligent creatures taught her much, including a great love of books and puzzles. But Lydia was troubled when no one believed her tales of midnight adventures. The solution was clear: she'd have to become a writer. Lydia opened Dangerous Visions, a science fiction bookstore, to ensure a steady supply of good reading material, then went on to write more than fifty animation scripts for shows you've undoubtedly watched, bought the toys for, and since forgotten. Lydia and her husband, Art Cover, live in Los Angeles with three dogs, six cats, and far too many books to read in one lifetime. Immortality seems the only option.

My favorite part of summer is

❏ anytime I'm not in the car.

❏ burying my dad in the sand while he's taking a nap.

❏ asking my mom "Are we having fun yet?" every five minutes and then telling her I was just reading the title of this cool activity book out loud.

Are We Having Fun Yet?

Summer Activities Inspired By

NICKELODEON MAGAZINE

Coming mid-May 1998

 A MINSTREL® BOOK

Published by Pocket Books

NICKELODEON/MINSTREL BOOKS POINTS PROGRAM

Official Rules

1. **HOW TO COLLECT POINTS:** Points may be collected by purchasing books in the following series, *The Secret World of Alex Mack*™, *Are You Afraid of the Dark?*™, and *The Mystery Files of Shelby Woo*™. Only books in the series published March 1998 and after are eligible for program. Points can be redeemed for merchandise by completing the coupons (found in the back of the books) and mailing with a check or money order in the exact amount to cover postage and handling to Nickelodeon/Minstrel Points Program, P.O. Box 7777-G140, Mt. Prospect, IL 60056-7777. Each coupon is worth 5 points. Copies of coupons are not valid. Simon & Schuster is not responsible for lost, late, illegible, incomplete, stolen, postage-due, or misdirected mail.

2. **40 POINT MINIMUM:** Each redemption request must contain a minimum of 40 points, or 8 coupons, in order to redeem for merchandise. Limit one merchandise request per envelope: 8 coupons (40 points), 12 coupons (60 points), 15 coupons (75 points), or 20 coupons (100 points).

3. **ELIGIBILITY:** Open to legal residents of the United States (excluding Puerto Rico) and Canada (excluding Quebec) only. Void where taxed, licensed, restricted, or prohibited by law. Redemption requests from groups, clubs, or organizations will not be honored.

4. **DELIVERY:** Allow 6-8 weeks for delivery of merchandise.

5. **MERCHANDISE:** All merchandise is subject to availability and may be replaced with an item of merchandise of equal or greater value at the sole discretion of Simon & Schuster.

6. **ORDER DEADLINE:** All redemption requests must be received by January 31, 1999, or while supplies last. Offer may not be combined with any other promotional offer from Simon & Schuster. Employees and the immediate family members of such employees of Simon & Schuster, its parent company, subsidiaries, divisions and related companies and their respective agencies and agents are ineligible to participate.

COMPLETE THE COUPON AND MAIL TO
NICKELODEON/MINSTREL POINTS PROGRAM
P.O. BOX 7777-G140
MT. PROSPECT, IL 60056-7777

NAME_____

ADDRESS_____

CITY _____ STATE _____ ZIP _____

THIS COUPON WORTH FIVE POINTS
Offer expires January 31, 1999

I have enclosed __ coupons and a check/money order (in U.S. currency only) made payable to "Nickelodeon/Minstrel Books Points Program" to cover postage and handling.

❑ 8 coupons (+ $3.50 postage and handling)   ❑ 15 coupons (+ $3.50 postage and handling)

❑ 12 coupons (+ $3.50 postage and handling)   ❑ 20 coupons (+ $5.50 postage and handling)

1464(2of2)